The Missing Barbegazi

H.S. NORUP was born in Denmark and lived in the US, the UK, Austria, and Switzerland before moving to Singapore. Now, she has returned to Switzerland with her husband and two teenage sons. This is Helle's debut novel and very much draws on her love of the Alps, her passion for skiing, and her belief that magic is all around us—particularly in the love, trust, and companionship found in families.

The Missing Barbegazi

H.S. Norup

JOLLY
FiSH
PRESS

Mendota Heights, Minnesota

The Missing Barbegazi was first published in Great Britain by Pushkin Press in 2018

Pushkin Children's
71–75 Shelton Street
London WC2H 9JQ
www.pushkinpress.com

Published by arrangement with Pushkin Press Limited through Rights People, London.

Published in the United States by Jolly Fish Press, an imprint of North Star Editions, Inc.

First US Edition
First US Printing, 2019

Book design by Sarah Taplin
Cover design by Sarah Taplin
Cover and interior illustration by Aubrey Blackham

Library of Congress Cataloging-in-Publication Data
Names: Norup, H. S., author.
Title: The missing barbegazi / by H. S. Norup.
Description: First US edition. | Mendota Heights, MN : Published in the
United States by Jolly Fish Press, an imprint of North Star Editions,
Inc., [2019] | "The missing barbegazi was first published in Great Britain
by Pushkin Press in 2018"—Copyright page. | Summary: While skiing in the
Alps, Tessa discovers and befriends Gawion, a mythical gnome-like creature
called a barbegazi, whose sister is missing and may have been captured by
humans.
Identifiers: LCCN 2019015358 (print) | LCCN 2019019210 (ebook) | ISBN
9781631633782 (ebook) | ISBN 9781631633775 (print)
Subjects: | CYAC: Animals, Mythical—Fiction. | Skis and skiing—Fiction. |
Avalanches—Fiction. | Alps—Fiction.
Classification: LCC PZ7.1.N657 (ebook) | LCC PZ7.1.N657 Mi 2019 (print) | DDC
[Fic]—dc23
LC record available at https://lccn.loc.gov/2019015358

Jolly Fish Press
North Star Editions, Inc.
2297 Waters Drive
Mendota Heights, MN 55120
www.jollyfishpress.com

Printed in the United States of America

For my three favorite skiers

MONDAY, DECEMBER 26

—1—

Tessa

Tessa aimed her binoculars at the white blanket of new snow, searching for a barbegazi. The T-bar lift pulled her uphill, along the boundary of the ski area, as she scanned the mountains on the far side of the gorge. Her skis wobbled over a bump, and the eyepiece knocked against her cheekbone. She winced, but kept her eyes fixed on a crevice, from where small chunks of snow were rolling down the smooth white slope. Had they been loosened by a barbegazi?

She itched to ski beyond the prepared slopes to get closer. But that was impossible. A blizzard had raged over Christmas, and the avalanche warning was high. Today, not even the craziest skiers braved the dangerous off-piste. Yet.

Tessa's view of the crevice became a gray blur when the lift dragged her into a cloud. Annoyed, she lowered the binoculars, and let them dangle from their strap. Everything beyond the red trousers and green jackets of her ski-club teammates on the T-bars in front vanished in the mist. The clamminess chilled her, and she pushed her long brown braids back, snuggled into her soft fleece, and thought about the barbegazi. If only she could find their caves in the snow, and see them surf on avalanches.

When she emerged above the cloud, stray snowflakes glittered in the sun, filling the air with magic gold dust. The brightness blinded her. She tugged down the goggles on her helmet until they protected her eyes.

Empty T-bars swung back and forth where the other two eleven-year-old girls from the racing team waited. While dismounting the lift, Tessa tried to jam the binoculars into her pocket.

"Looking for fairies again?" Maria called out.

"They're not fairies," Tessa mumbled through the glove she had in her mouth, while she closed the zipper on her bulky pocket. She hoped Coach wouldn't notice. "They're—"

"Whatever." Maria exchanged a glance with Lisa. "It's not like anyone's ever seen one. Or will."

"My opa has." Tessa pointed with her ski pole toward the gully, on the other side of the T-bar lift. "It rescued him down—"

"Nobody believed your grandfather."

Her throat tightened, at Maria's harsh interruption.

"Everyone knows they're extinct, Tessa." Lisa's tone was friendlier than Maria's. Perhaps she was also remembering Opa's funeral.

Not trusting her voice to sound steady, Tessa just shook her head.

"Oh my God, Tessa." Maria waved her arms wildly and

pointed toward the mountainside beyond the gully. "Look! Quick."

Was something moving up there again? Tessa couldn't help turning.

"I thought they were extinct. But, no, I see one. It's a..." Maria drew a long, deep breath. "A-a-a... T. rex!"

Both she and Lisa exploded into fits of giggles.

"Very funny," Tessa muttered. Hidden behind the goggles, tears welled up in her eyes. "Don't wait. I need the restroom," she said, trying not to sound choked up, and she started gliding over to the mountain hut.

Still giggling, Maria set off, and Lisa followed her new best friend.

The lump in Tessa's throat grew. She didn't need the toilet, and she didn't really care what they thought. She missed Opa so much her chest hurt. The pain pulsed into her heart as if all the blood in her body was trying to fill an Opa-shaped hole. No wonder Oma was ill, if this kind of pain was attacking her weak heart.

Tessa stopped and looked back to where Maria had pointed for her dinosaur prank. Above it, by a rocky outcrop, a small movement caught her eye. She gasped. Something white was bouncing up the snowy slope, then disappeared behind the rock. It definitely wasn't a skier. Could it be a barbegazi?

Without taking her eyes off the outcrop, she fish-boned her way back up the slope, past the swinging T-bars and the top station of the lift. Here, on the crest of Kapall, orange netting barred the way out onto the ridge and the untamed part of the mountains. Tessa tried looking through the binoculars, but the outcrop obstructed her view of where she'd seen the creature last. If she could just get a bit nearer…

A ski-route-closed sign warned of alpine danger. Tessa checked to make sure that none of her teammates were looking. If anyone saw her ski off-piste in these conditions, Coach would ban her from training, and Mum would lock her skis away forever.

And she wasn't going to ski off-piste. Not really. The first stretch of the ski route, through the gully and into the gorge, was almost flat, and she'd turn back as soon as she'd had a peek behind that outcrop.

With a last glance back, she squeezed through a gap between the nets, and out into the deep snow.

The wind had blown most of the snow away from the top of the ridge, and Tessa glided effortlessly along the flat surface. More of the crevice behind the outcrop came into view. To gain a better perspective, she planted her poles into the snow and stepped nearer to the edge. She looked through her binoculars.

There was a blurry spot on one of the lenses. Without taking off her glove, she rummaged in her pocket for a tissue, and one of the lens covers fell out. Instinctively, Tessa leaned down to grab it.

Under her sudden, shifting weight, the ground beneath her right ski disappeared, as the snow overhang she had edged onto broke apart. A reflex sent both her arms outward, to help her balance. The binocular-strap jerked at her neck as she let go of them. Tessa threw all her weight onto her left ski, but it was sliding sideways toward the drop... then stopped with a screech, on a flat rock that was sticking out of the snow.

Tessa's breaths came in sharp gulps. She balanced on her left leg. It shook with the effort.

Stupid. Stupid. Stupid. How many times had Opa told her to watch out for overhangs after a storm?

Below her hovering right ski, the bulk of snow she'd released was now tumbling down the mountainside, gathering speed and volume, and growing into a mini avalanche.

When she lowered her right leg, only a narrow strip of the ski rested on solid ground. She'd not slid far, but her ski poles were beyond reach. What could she do?

If she jumped the drop and landed on both feet, she could ski down the steep slope. She'd done it before with Opa. Though not from this height. Not with this much new snow. And never alone.

Instead, with the carefulness of a tightrope walker, she shifted her weight to the right ski, testing its hold on the rock. It held. In slow motion, she lifted the left ski a tiny bit and pushed it left. She balanced, shifted her weight and continued, lifting one ski at a time, very slowly inching away from the edge.

When she had made it to the other side of her ski poles, she collapsed on the snow, sobbing. Her whole body quivered. Only now did she dare to think what might have happened if both her skis had been on the overhang.

After Tessa stopped shaking, she hauled herself back to the

ski area. By the barrier nets, she paused and looked back at the outcrop. Had she imagined the movement earlier, or really seen a barbegazi?

As she turned round, she collided with a tall man in a white ski outfit, a white helmet, and mirrored goggles, who was pushing through the gap in the nets. He grabbed her arm.

"Watch where you're going," he snarled, his teeth gritted below a pale wispy mustache, which was so thin it looked like a pair of frowning eyebrows.

"Sorry." Tessa wrenched her jacket out of his hold.

The man skied along the ridge, past the breach Tessa had made in the overhang, before he disappeared down the steep decline into the gully.

All in white. How stupid. No one would ever find him if he got caught in an avalanche.

2

Gawion

Gawion was too hungry and too warm to wait for the avalanche any longer. He left his sister below the most unstable-looking snow cornice, and traversed the steep mountainside to their cave entrance. After wrapping his long beard round his neck three times, he dived down into the hole and propelled himself through the narrow snow tunnel. His enormous foot got stuck when he forgot to twist it at a bend, but two paddling kicks soon enlarged the tunnel and freed his foot. He arrived home, sliding on his belly.

"Ahh, it is awfully nice and chilly in here," he said. His eyes adjusted to the dim light, and he hurried over to the huge chunk of glacier ice in the center of the cozy cave. Pointing his feet outward, he leaned his whole body against it to absorb the coldness. Papa sat on a smaller cube of ice around the other side, with Liel on his knees. They both stretched their furry hands toward the blue ice. Gawion had once sneaked down to the village after dark and seen humans sit in exactly the same way in front of flames.

Next, he lay down on his back and shuffled the soles of his long feet up to the glacier ice cooler. Only the claws on the ends of his toes stuck out above it.

"Gawion!" his mother screeched. "You have soiled my newly snowed floor."

"Sorry, Maman." He began picking up the pine needles and moss that had come off his fur and dirtied the floor.

With a swish, Maman swung her long beard over her shoulder, so she would not stumble on it, and marched back into the eating cave. Gawion followed her, hungry as always. This smaller cave was closest to the rock face, and the cascading icicles of a frozen waterfall decorated the back wall. He threw the dirt into a crack between the snowy floor and the gleaming ice.

Gawion scooped a handful of snow out of the wall next to the waterfall—his favorite flavor of snow inside the cluster of linked caves—and stuffed it into his mouth. The tiny crystals prickled his tongue. He munched and sucked on them with loud smacking noises. This snow had the delicious taste of a particularly icy snowstorm.

"Are there any raspberries?" he asked.

"Stop talking with your mouth full." Maman sighed. She looked tired, and her eyes had a faint, sun-colored tint around their sky-blue center. "We are out of raspberries. You can have one blackberry."

She carefully removed the shard of ice in front of their berry store, picked a large one from the tiny pile inside, and popped it into his mouth. Gawion savored it, sucking on the hard, frozen lump until it dissolved into the tart juice of a not-quite-ripe forest blackberry.

"Where is Maegorodiel?" she asked, glancing over his head into the other cave.

"Waiting for an avalanche," Gawion said. "Only, I was hungry…"

"How could you leave her? There might still be humans about!"

"Maman, we are one-hundred-and-fifty-four years old."

Just then they heard a shrill whistle. A loud rumble followed it, and flakes fell from the ceiling. Finally, the avalanche he had been waiting for. And he had missed it.

"Potzblitz! Why is Maeg always lucky?" As usual, he should have listened to his twin sister.

Maman had closed the berry store, so he returned to the main cave, where Liel nestled into Papa's beard.

Gawion could not be bothered getting fresh snow for the floor, so he swept his foot sideways, hiding the remaining pine needles, while he looked over his shoulder to check his mother was not watching.

"Papa, tell the story of how you escaped from the zoo," Liel murmured, half asleep.

From somewhere outside, three piercing whistles could be heard. The third whistle was cut off and lacked the urgency of the first two, but left no doubt this was a desperate cry for help.

"Maeg!" Maman screamed.

Papa sprang up. Liel toppled over, hit the ice cooler, and

began wailing. Gawion scrambled through the tunnel behind Papa.

Outside, the trail of a huge avalanche stretched out below them, all the way into the gorge the humans called "Schöngraben." A few times they had dug human corpses out of avalanches there, and he had wondered why naming a place something that sounded like "beautiful grave" had not been sufficient warning.

Gawion chased his father down the mountain, surfing on the snow. They swerved on overhangs, hoping they might start new avalanches to carry them downward even faster. Where they reached the end of the avalanche's long tongue, the ground flattened. An assortment of boulders lay scattered in front of it, like gigantic, frozen blackberries spat from the mouth of the gully. They whistled for Maeg while they searched underneath and around each one. The snow posed no danger to Maeg, but if she had somehow hit her head on a boulder... That was what Papa said, at least. Gawion wondered how Maeg could have whistled the emergency signal if she had been knocked out, and how she could have been knocked out in the first place. She was even better than him at surfing the avalanches.

Papa's whistling calls moved farther away from Gawion as they continued their search. Gawion had no problems seeing in the dark, but, trying to look everywhere at once, he stumbled into a hollow in the snow.

He sniffed, smelling all the different snow types the avalanche had carried. There was a whiff of thawing spring snow too—the sweet scent of Maeg.

"Maeg, where are you?" he called, and began digging.

But then his large nose caught something else. A pungent stench that gave him a scalding, trickling sensation down his spine. The snow around him reeked of iron.

He whistled for Papa to come, while he groped around in the loose snow. When Papa appeared, he had just found a handful of barbegazi fur.

Without speaking, he handed it to his father.

Papa gasped and said, "She has been taken, I fear."

FROM *HABITS & HABITATS:*
A HISTORIC ACCOUNT OF ALPINE
ELVES BY PROFESSOR
DR. EBERHART LUDWIG
FRITZ BAHNE

———————

Barbegazi are mountain elves, although humans often mistake them for dwarfs, due to their short, stout stature. A mature barbegazi of approximately three hundred years in age can reach a height of 1.2 meters, roughly the size of an average seven-year-old. Fully grown, they weigh around ten kilograms— less than half that of a similar-sized human child.

This lightness and low density, combined with their enormous feet, enable them to "surf" on avalanches.

TUESDAY, DECEMBER 27

3

Tessa

Tessa had forgotten to get her skis serviced. Again. So she began the training session with Coach on a bad note.

If him yelling "Those skis'd better be like new tomorrow or you can take them down to the sawmill, borrow a chainsaw, turn them into splinters, make a bonfire in your garden, and forget about the race on Saturday!" without taking a breath could be called merely a bad note.

Tessa just stared at the ground. The race meant nothing to her any more. Yesterday, when Aunt Annie dropped off some homemade goulash soup, she'd overheard her talking to Mum about Oma. Mum had cried. From the gap left open by the kitchen door, Tessa had glimpsed Mum's thin, convulsing shoulders as she was embraced by Aunt Annie's pudgy arms.

"What if she gives up?" Mum sobbed. "This article I read said if one spouse dies, the other might lose the will to go on. Especially around Christmas."

Aunt Annie murmured something that Tessa couldn't hear

because blood was pounding in her ears and surging toward her chest. The thought of having two holes to try and fill in her heart made her run to her room, and hide in the soft fluff of her pillow.

"Your turn, Miss My-head's-in-the-clouds," Coach yelled. "And stay active. Bend your knees. Don't sit like you're at a tea party."

Tessa nodded, without looking up, and got into starting position between the long stakes that marked the beginning of the training course. She planted her poles into the snow and leaned back, flexing her knee and hip joints, tensing her muscles. On the piste in front of her, giant slalom gates were positioned in a colorful zigzag.

"Three, two, one, go!"

At "Go" Tessa catapulted herself forward and pushed off with both poles three times. Then she crouched, and, shifting her weight, raced through the maze of red and blue gates.

"Knees, Tessa!" Coach shouted from behind.

The dull metal edges of her skis had little hold on the snow, and she slid sideways in the turns. Cold air slipped under the rim of Tessa's helmet, whistling in her ears. If only she could hear a barbegazi whistle. Opa had told her they whistled warnings, signaling avalanches.

A figure in green stood waving their arms just ahead of her. Tessa canted her skis, sending a shower of powdery snow over Karen, the assistant coach, who'd stopped her in the middle of the run.

"Wake up, Tessa! The U12 competition will be tough this year. You need to up your game. Like Lisa and Maria." When Karen shook her head, fine white dust fell from her striped, knitted hat.

After crossing the finish line, Tessa zoomed in and out between hesitant tourists and caterpillar-like ski-school groups, to the lift. She arrived just as Lisa and Maria got on either side of a T-bar, whispering and giggling.

On the next run, she botched the start, didn't find her rhythm, and missed a gate. At the top of the course, Coach swore. She conveniently overlooked Karen's waving arms.

The rest of the morning was like climbing a mountain of ice. Blindfolded. Wearing slippers.

Heavy clouds pressed down on the Alps, concealing the peaks and becoming one with the snow-covered slopes. The lift rides were a complete waste of time—everywhere Tessa pointed her binoculars showed the same gray blur. Besides, the avalanche risk had gone down, and today tourists crowded the off-piste. The barbegazi had to be in hiding.

After her final run, Felix slid up beside her in the queue, and they shared a T-bar back to the top. They were second cousins, but he was almost like a brother to her. Felix was also the best skier in the team.

"Did you see that?" he asked, while they settled on the orange bar. "What a save! My approach to the last red gate was all wrong, but then I took the turn on my inside ski and threw my weight forward and knocked the gate away with my shoulder."

"Cool," Tessa said. She hadn't seen his run.

"And my catapult start... I wanna do it exactly like that on Saturday. Still three more training days left before the first race, and I'm ready!" Felix pushed his sleeve up to look at his sports watch. "Yes! My pulse is already down. D'you have something to eat? I'm starving. I hope there's still some of Mum's goulash left over."

"Don't count on it. She brought that over for me and Oma yesterday. But I doubt you'll starve." Aunt Annie—who wasn't actually Tessa's aunt, but married to Mum's cousin Harry—was known throughout the whole village for her delicious food and cakes.

"What's that? Is it chocolate?" Felix poked at her bulging pocket.

"Just my binoculars."

"You're not still looking for those...you know... Great Uncle Willy's barbie-fairy-thingies?"

"Not barbies. A barbegazi. One saved him after an avalanche. Right down there." Tessa jabbed her pole toward Schöngraben. "Opa said he'd show me, but now he's gone, and—" She stopped speaking before the lump in her throat could choke her voice.

They'd been picking berries in the gully when Opa pointed and said: "The barbegazi dug me out of the avalanche over there. Come December, I'll show you." Munching on blueberries, she'd glanced up from the bush for a second. Had he planned to show her a barbegazi, or just the spot?

Tessa speared a clump of snow with her pole, making it

crumble. "And your grandfather didn't even believe his own brother."

The track turned bumpy on a steep stretch. Tessa concentrated on her skis not crossing, and they glided side by side in awkward silence.

After a while, Felix said, "One of our guests, a regular, was in an avalanche down there yesterday afternoon. It was weird—"

"Did they save him?"

"Who? Those barbie-things? Come on, Tessa. But it was so weird. He never talks to anyone, and he's only interested in the avalanche report. A fanatic off-piste skier. Has all the coolest equipment. Even that new electrical avalanche airbag…"

She knew just the type. A young guy with multicolored ski overalls, perhaps a ponytail. Probably Scandinavian.

"…Then last night he's all chatty, telling me about the avalanche, and afterward, going up the stairs, he whistled!"

"He whistled? That's what they do, you know."

"Who?"

"The barbegazi. Before avalanches, they whistle."

"So now you think he's one?" Felix gave a quick shake of his head. They'd reached the top, and he sped off, shouting that he wanted one last run.

Yeah, right. He just couldn't get away fast enough. Coach had already been dismantling the course when they passed it on the lift. They'd both seen that.

Tessa slid down to help clear the training piste, red-green streaks overtaking her.

If only she could find a barbegazi and prove they weren't extinct. It would solve all her problems. And everyone would know Opa had told the truth. That was bound to make Oma happy.

—4—

Gawion

They searched all night. Whistling, digging, probing, digging, whistling.

First, they sifted through the loose snow, where Gawion had discovered the barbegazi fur, and combed the rest of the avalanche trail, finding nothing.

"She cannot have been taken," Papa said again and again. "She must have had an accident. A blow to the head... A minor injury... We shall find her farther up the mountain."

But Gawion had not mistaken the stench of iron in the hollow where he found the fur. Unfortunately, Papa had neither smelled thawing spring snow nor iron, and Gawion cursed himself for having scattered the snow before Papa arrived, making the scents disperse.

Papa took him across the flattened, rippled snow that attracted flocks of humans during the day. A huge metal monster growled like a thousand angry dogs, and chased them up a steep slope with its light beams.

Fear made heat flash through Gawion and cramp the muscles of his sensitive soles. Terrified, he leapt over a sun-colored net, escaping into a ravine.

"Maeg cannot be here," Papa said, wide-eyed and shaking, before they slunk back to Schöngraben.

Where the ragged peaks rose naked above the snow, Gawion and Papa explored nooks and crannies, and sniffed behind boulders, looking in places Maeg had never been to. Gawion slid down couloirs and gullies and crawled back up them, making sure he overlooked nothing. Papa followed him, double-checking.

They stayed outside, exposed, long after daybreak, until the strange mechanical structures began transporting humans up the mountains again.

After Gawion had dozed for a while, he was fully rested and impatient to continue the search. He crept through the tunnel and peeked outside. Low clouds blocked the warmth of the sun and made it easy to hide from the humans. He could not even see the nearest of their mountain transporters, although the wind brought a faint echo of its sinister, metallic noise and distant human yells. But, today, he was not allowed to leave the cave on his own.

Back inside, Gawion lay down, close to the ice cooler. Liel was playing with the feathers she had gathered before the first big snowfall, oblivious to the worry around her.

His parents' muffled voices traveled through the snow wall from their resting cave. Maman's sobs and occasional shrieks— "We should never have stayed, Aeglosben… do not belong here…

carried those twins for nine winters… Home in Mont Blanc's sea of ice would have been safe"—were clearly audible above Papa's indistinct murmurs.

Gawion crept to the wall and pressed his ear against it. Papa had now raised his voice, saying, "Safe? Mont Blanc was never safe. They captured us there." This was a story he had told his children many times. It was also the reason Papa had been so quick to assume Maeg had been taken.

More than a century before Gawion was born, Papa, not quite awake after the summer sleep, had wandered into a trap. When his desperate whistles alerted Maman and her father, they tried to rescue him. But the humans had attacked them with iron chains, and captured all three barbegazi. After traveling for a moon in an iron cage on a cart, they had arrived at Schönbrunn Palace in Vienna. Here they were gifted to the Empress Maria Theresa and, as part of the imperial menagerie, treated like royalty. Imprisoned royalty.

"We are much safer here," Papa said, trying to persuade Maman that his initial fear of an abduction had been foolish. Maeg could not have been captured. No one could have taken her, because no one knew a barbegazi family lived in these mountains.

Well, that was not entirely true. The berry-human knew about them. And that was Gawion's fault too. Just like it was his fault Maeg was gone. Potzblitz! If only he had stayed and waited for that avalanche, then they would know what had happened to Maeg.

When Maman appeared, he sprang up and followed her into the eating cave.

"Are we going out to search now? I am hungry."

"Blueberry or blackberry?" Maman sounded tired. "I shall give you one of each. And no one is leaving until nightfall."

As she stooped to pick up the berries, Gawion saw that the bald patch at the back of her head had grown since he first noticed it a few days ago. She looked shabbier and even thinner than she did after sleeping for a whole summer.

"Give these two to Liel." She stroked his beard. "Papa and I have already taken our dinner."

That did not sound right. Maman and Papa had not been outside the resting cave all morning. And the last few days, his parents had always been doing something else while the children ate. Were they eating at all? Or was that another reason for Maman's exhaustion?

"Are the rest of our berries on ice somewhere?" He snuffled, trying to catch a whiff of berries that might be hidden under the snow.

"Do not worry about that," Maman said. "Just find Maeg."

But he did worry. The winter solstice had come and gone, without the anticipated gift of berries from the human he had once saved. There was nowhere to find berries at this time of year. Except in the village. No matter what Papa thought, they might soon have several reasons to go near the humans. Perhaps Gawion should seek out the berry-human.

"Go on." Maman took his hand and placed the four berries in his palm.

Gawion put the blueberry into his mouth with a cube of ice, attempting to dilute the flavor and make it last longer. He maneuvered both lumps under his tongue, and fought the urge to swallow. His stomach growled.

5

Tessa

At home after ski training, Tessa skipped down the wooden stairs to the granny flat, with the bread she'd bought at the bakery and Aunt Annie's plastic container.

"Omaaaa," she called, opening the door. A musty smell met her, mixed with the scent of chamomile tea from the kitchen corner. The heavy curtains were opened, but the gray light from outside hardly made it past Oma's squishy armchairs, so Tessa switched on the ceiling lamp. At the far end of the room, the grandfather clock, next to the massive bookcase with all Opa's skiing trophies, ticked in rhythm with light snores from the sofa. Here, a magazine crossword puzzle covered part of Oma's pale face, and her glasses balanced on the tip of her nose. The checkered wool blanket had slid to the floor.

But it was too early for an afternoon nap.

On her knees, by the sofa, Tessa leaned in to hug Oma awake. She put her head on Oma's chest and listened to her heart. It beat much faster than the clock, and it didn't sound particularly weak.

Oma stroked Tessa's hair and whispered, "How was the snow?"

Tessa smiled. Every lunchtime in winter that was always the first question Oma had asked Opa. But she used to be bustling around with pots and pans, preparing lunch for the two hungry skiers—or one hungry skier and one hungry schoolgirl—when she asked it.

She almost answered "Not worth getting out of bed for," as Opa would've on a day like today, though she'd never seen him stay in bed.

"Okay, I guess," she said, and rose.

In the kitchen corner, she emptied the goulash soup into a saucepan and heated it over a low heat, as Aunt Annie had instructed. By the time it bubbled, she'd set the table, sliced the bread, and helped Oma get up.

She gulped down two portions before Oma had swallowed more than a few bites.

"You have to eat," Tessa said in Mum's voice. "You love Aunt Annie's goulash soup."

Oma leaned back and touched her lips with a napkin. "I must have eaten too much at breakfast."

That was a lie. There was only a teacup in the sink from this morning, but Tessa just nodded. She cleared the table, leaving the dishes for Mum to do when she came home between her lunch shift and dinner shift at the restaurant. Until then, Tessa would do her best to cheer Oma up.

"Do you want to play Rummy? Or I can get Scrabble from upstairs?"

Oma heaved herself up and shuffled back to the sofa.

"I think I need to lie down for a bit," she replied. "Why don't you tell me about today's skiing?"

Like Opa used to do. Tessa couldn't remember ever seeing Oma on skis, but, from Opa's daily reports, she knew the ski area better than most locals. They were dangerously close to talking about Opa. Was that a good idea? Mum had told her to avoid drama and anything that might be upsetting.

Tessa perched sideways on the edge of the sofa. Suddenly it seemed that every topic led to Opa. She couldn't say her skis needed service without both of them thinking how Opa used to sharpen and wax her skis. The avalanche yesterday had been near Opa's avalanche. Even her problems with the other girls were linked to the barbegazi, and from them, to Opa.

"What is it, dear?" Oma took her hand and gave it a soft squeeze. "I'm not made of glass just because my ticker's acting up."

"It's…" Oma might be the only person in the whole world who knew the barbegazi weren't extinct. Perhaps they could talk about them without mentioning Opa.

Oma's thumb stroked Tessa's hand, teasing the words out.

"It's the barbegazi. Nobody believes they still exist."

The thumb strokes stopped. "You mean, nobody believed your grandfather."

"Did you?" Tessa asked quietly.

"Of course I did. He survived an avalanche that flattened two rows of trees, and somehow he made it home on a broken leg. Your grandfather—rest his soul—had no patience for fantasy. He could never have imagined the barbegazi."

Oma let go of Tessa's hand. She found the handkerchief hidden in her sleeve and dabbed at her eyes, but she spoke with more force than Tessa had heard in a long time.

"Until that professor came, he didn't even know they were called barbegazi."

"What professor?"

"The author of that fairy book. Even mentioned Opa in the barbegazi chapter. The two of you were always looking at it when you were little. Don't you remember?"

Shaking her head, Tessa walked over to the bookcase, and scanned the heavy, dark-green and wine-red hardbacks.

"Try behind my knitting basket," Oma said.

On the bottom shelf, squeezed in after volumes nineteen to thirty of the encyclopedia, stood a thin black book.

Tessa pried it out. Seeing it, she vaguely remembered drawings of elves, and sitting by the fire upstairs, listening to Opa's story. She'd been too young to read, but he always showed her the section about him. This would be proof. Lisa and Maria could see for themselves that Opa had told the truth.

A bookmark stuck out in the middle, and her trembling hands opened it there. The font was small, and Opa's notes and a pencil-sketched barbegazi filled the margins. A big arrow pointed to the place she was looking for, and she read:

Over the years, several skiers caught in avalanches claim to have been dug out by something white and hairy. However, as the persons were unconscious when found by rescue teams, none of their stories have credibility.

As late as last year, a skier reported his miraculous rescue in the Arlberg region of Austria. Despite the fact that Arlberg is several hundred kilometers from any historical sightings of barbegazi, which were all near major glaciers in the Swiss and French Alps, this author traveled to the region to investigate. Unfortunately, the skier, Willy Berger, withdrew his story of the sighting, confessing to have suffered a serious head trauma, with resulting hallucinations, in the avalanche.

Head trauma. Hallucinations. This was all wrong. Opa had always told her a barbegazi saved his life. Why would he say something else to this author?

Tessa slumped into a squishy armchair, across from the sofa where Oma lay with her eyes closed. It didn't prove anything. But she still believed Opa. Whoever had written this book had misunderstood. She closed it and tried to decipher the name on the spine. The tiny letters there, once golden, had lost their color and become dark shadows. Inside the cover, curly writing said: *Habits & Habitats: A Historic Account of Alpine Elves by Professor Dr. Eberhart Ludwig Fritz Bahne.*

What a strange name! She entered it in the search engine on her phone, and tapped the first result. It was from the Institute of Zoology at the University of Zurich. A long list of Professor Bahne's publications appeared. She scrolled down, stopping to read interesting titles, like *Animal Behavior: Dying Elfish Customs* and *On the Origin of Elves: Survival of the Least Humanoid* and *Secrets of the Glaciers: Proof Against Barbegazi Extinction?*

At that last one, Tessa jumped up.

Oma stirred. "Did you say something, dear?"

She wanted to do a happy dance, but stopped herself. Mum had said no drama.

"That professor believes they're alive," she replied, as calmly as possible.

Outside, on the snow-covered garden table, tiny flecks landed at irregular intervals. The clock chimed. Two thirty. Mum would be home soon.

"Sorry, Oma. I forgot… Tell Mum I went skiing with… Erm…"

"Mmm hmm," Oma murmured, with closed eyes.

For a moment, Tessa watched her still shape, reluctant to leave. She spread the blanket over Oma's stockinged legs, before she ran upstairs, hugging the book against her chest. *A-live-a-live-a-live*, her steps tramped.

Of course, the barbegazi had survived. And she'd find them, if she searched in the right spot.

FROM *HABITS & HABITATS: A HISTORIC ACCOUNT OF ALPINE ELVES* BY PROFESSOR DR. EBERHART LUDWIG FRITZ BAHNE

The name *barbegazi* comes from the French *barbe glacée,* meaning "frozen beard."

The white beards of grown males often reach the ground. Female beards are slightly shorter. Both females and males use their beards as scarves, but whether the beards have other functions as well is unknown.

Similar to other species of elves, barbegazi have pointed ears, iron intolerance, and limited magical abilities.

6

Tessa

Tessa dismounted the chairlift on the crest of Kapall, next to the barrier nets she'd slipped through yesterday. The ski route was open today, and the nets rolled back. On her way up, she'd thought about Professor Bahne. His email address was listed on the Institute of Zoology website. It was perfect. After she found a barbegazi, she'd write to him, then he could mention her in one of his books, and everyone would believe her.

Dark clouds swelled over the Arlberg pass, and snow fell in big fluffy lumps. The cold lift had frozen her bottom. Tessa shivered. To get warm, she started out with short, quick turns— Coach would've been pleased. She sped past the deserted training area in tuck position, taking advantage of the empty piste, and stopped by the edge of the traverse path that led back to the chairlift. The place Opa had shown her, where he'd been rescued, was below the Törli couloir, near the mountain stream. At least, that's how she remembered it.

Half-erased tracks snaked their way down the white surface,

disappearing into the clouds above Schöngraben. The off-piste skiers from this morning were gone—probably finishing their days with après-ski drinks and music, in mountain huts. That was both good—the barbegazi wouldn't need to hide—and bad: no one would be near to help if anything happened to her. No one even knew where she was, and, on its own, her avalanche transceiver was pointless.

Tessa hesitated. She searched the contacts on her phone for someone to tell where she was headed. Lisa: no, Felix: no, Coach: definitely no, Dad—he lived thousands of kilometers away—no, no, no. She wasn't allowed to ski off-piste alone. Mum would be livid, if she ever found out. Felix was a better option than the other contacts, and his dad, Uncle Harry, was a rescue patrol volunteer.

She tapped with her frozen fingers: I ski Schöngraben now :-).

After pressing send, she donned her gloves, and left the prepared slopes. The ski route began easy and flat, following the forest, above the tree line. Her phone beeped, but she didn't stop. She only paused to catch her breath, where the landscape changed and the slope steepened.

Every season, the first time she stood on the edge of this near-vertical drop, it unnerved her. Only the knowledge that she'd survived the descent in earlier years assured her she could do it again. Normally, the bottom of Schöngraben was visible, but today it was snowing so much the view was grayed-out.

Turning back was still possible. She only needed to backtrack up to the trail through the forest. A route she'd often taken last year with Lisa.

After a long look at the whirling snow above the shrouded gorge, she made up her mind. The barbegazi would still be there tomorrow. She turned and shuffled sideways, up toward the trail. The soft snow made it hard work, and she soon became warm and sweaty inside her ski jacket.

A piercing whistle resonated between the mountainsides.

Tessa stopped dead. The hairs on the back of her neck stood up. The strange whistle sounded again, from high up on the opposite ridge. A similar peculiar whistle answered, from deep below in Schöngraben. The penetrating whistles didn't sound like rescue whistles, or referee whistles, or the shrill tone from blowing hard in the top part of the wooden recorders in the music room, or anything else she'd ever heard.

In an instant, she changed her decision and skied back down the slope. After five turns, she'd passed the spot where she'd begun backtracking, and, on the steep drop, there was no turning back. The barbegazi would save her if she was caught in an avalanche, wouldn't they?

They didn't whistle again. Silence cushioned her, like cotton wool. The only sounds were the clanks of her skis, whenever they grazed each other, and her wheezing breaths. The ground flattened out. Her turns became effortless. She floated across the white blanket, almost without touching it, until something blocked her skis. They stopped abruptly and Tessa flew in a low arc, landing face down in soft, wet snow.

Both skis remained attached—the bindings were tightened for race practice. She got up and brushed the snow away. Huge, boulder-sized snow heaps surrounded her. The remains of yesterday's avalanche. It had come down through the narrow Törli couloir, the other ski route in Schöngraben. The only route Opa had forbidden her to ski. The route where an avalanche had once buried him.

Somewhere nearby, he'd met the barbegazi.

Tessa edged forward, taking care to avoid the snow-covered rocks, while she searched for something resembling a barbegazi cave entrance. Snow stuck to her goggles, blocking her vision, although she kept wiping it away. She couldn't see the end of Schöngraben, where two massive man-made earth mounds protected the village from avalanches. The place where she should cross the mountain stream must be close by. Was she too far to the right? Or had she crossed already? This was so stupid. What did she think she was doing, following the sound of whistles? They could've been anything. Anywhere. Echoes in the mountains often made sound appear to be coming from a completely different direction. Perhaps it had been the whistle from a train down in the valley. How silly to think she'd heard a barbegazi!

She'd lost her speed, and she had to push herself through the deep snow. Her sweaty thermal underwear turned cold, making her shudder. The falling fluff swallowed the sound of her hiccupping sobs. Tears gathered inside her goggles. She could see even less while crying.

Suddenly, the ground below her caved in, revealing a hidden

hollow under the new snow. Tessa tried to scramble back, but it was too late.

The tips of her skis rose, while her weight tilted her back. Something in her stomach somersaulted. She screamed. Windmilling her arms and the ski poles, she seemed to hover, suspended for an instant. Then the tails of her skis hit the ground. Both ski bindings released, catapulting her backward, and she landed, with a crunch, on her back protector. Her helmet touched down, bouncing once. She tried to breathe, but the air had been knocked out of her.

A quiet, "Help," escaped her. And then she just lay at the bottom of the hole.

Far above, snow whirled out of the dark gray sky.

—7—

Gawion

They crawled outside before the noisy metal things stopped. A snowstorm was coming. Papa said none of the humans would be foolish enough to journey through Schöngraben with so poor visibility. Even Maman and Liel came out to search near the cave.

Gawion surfed over to the western forest. He bounded up the steep scarp, between two rows of fir trees. Bending his toes so his claws gripped, and bouncing his heels off the ground, he propelled himself upward. Then he slid downhill between the next two rows. All the while, searching for signs of his sister. But he found nothing.

Papa wanted them to comb the forests on both flanks of the gorge, although the avalanche trail ran straight between them.

"If she is injured, she might not be able to dig herself out of the snow," Papa had said, as if that was what he really believed. "Perhaps she has even gone into deep sleep to preserve energy, and cannot hear us."

Gawion had tried to tell Papa that Maeg must be below the

avalanche tongue, because it was clear from her first whistle that she had been surfing the avalanche. But Papa refused to think rationally.

Despite the emergency whistle, the lump of her fur, and Gawion having smelled iron, Papa refused to believe Maeg had been abducted, which was like someone denying winter was ending when the mountain streams overflowed and patches of bright grass appeared in the snow.

They ought to search much nearer to the human habitats, but Papa had forbidden Gawion to pass through the human-made earth mounds at the end of the narrow valley. Perhaps he could sneak around them to the village instead.

Almost as if he knew what Gawion was considering, Papa whistled from somewhere above, in the eastern forest. A second check-up whistle sounded, before Gawion answered.

He zigzagged up and down, trawling the forest. The snow-fall covered his tracks, so at least he need not worry about that. His stomach growled again and again. Might he find a few late blackberries under the snow on a north-facing stretch?

The mere thought of berries made his mouth water. He grabbed a handful of snow and sucked on it, hoping to satisfy his hunger. It was no good. The powdery snow lacked taste and density. It disappeared on his tongue without even cooling his mouth.

He reached the bottom again, close to the mountain stream. It gurgled deep below the snow. The pit he had dug was nearby. If only the berry-human had finally delivered the gift.

He was gliding toward the hole when he heard a scream. A scream, not a whistle. And a very soft, human "Help."

Helping humans did not interest him, right now. But if a human had captured Maeg, perhaps he should capture a human.

The idea was ridiculous. Humans could not survive in the snow half as long as barbegazi could survive non-freezing temperatures, which was not very long.

When the deep hole he had dug for the berries came into view, he hurried toward it, then stopped. What if Maeg's abductor was down there? Perhaps it had set a barbegazi trap. Should he run and hide? Or let himself be captured to find out where it had taken Maeg?

Gawion inched closer to the hole.

8

Tessa

Tessa swallowed gulps of air. She had stopped crying. Her situation was simply too scary for tears. Instead, she pushed her goggles up and wiped her eyes. She wasn't buried under the snow, but this was the next worst thing.

The deep, cave-like hole was roundish and several meters across. The gap in the overhanging snow above her was much smaller—Tessa-sized, plus the bit her floundering poles and skis had torn down. Rounded rocks broke through the bumpy ground. This place wasn't cozy, not like the barbegazi caves in her imagination.

Standing and stretching, she thrust one ski pole upward. It barely reached the opening. Climbing up the soft snow wall seemed impossible. There was a gap in the wall, a sort of tunnel, that led into the snow. It was dark and narrow. Perhaps she could worm her way through it. But where would it end?

She took her phone out. No connection. Not even a single little bar. Mum's old phone, and it was useless. The cracked screen showed two texts. One was from Mum: **Home with Oma. Off to work soon. Have fun with Lisa. Mum xxx.** The other was from Felix. **U r crazy:-(:-0**, it read. He'd sent it two minutes after she'd texted him.

A sob escaped her. Mum wouldn't worry, if she thought Tessa was at Lisa's. She'd just think the girls were having one of their sleepovers. Like they used to. When would Felix begin to worry and tell Uncle Harry? Would Felix worry at all? He'd probably be lost in a computer game and only wonder where she was when she didn't turn up for ski training tomorrow. She stifled another sob. No one would be looking for her!

She had to do something. Find a way out, or make some kind of sign. The piste patrol only supervised the prepared slopes, but if, against all odds, someone came this way, they would not detect the signal from her avalanche transceiver unless they searched for it. She picked up one of her skis, held it with both hands over her shoulder, and threw it. The ski flew out of the hole and disappeared. She crossed her gloved fingers, hoping it had landed upright, sticking out of the snow like a signpost.

The other ski, when she tried throwing it, landed on the edge, ripping more snow down, before it crashed to the ground. That gave her an idea. Using the ski, she hacked her way round the rim, enlarging the opening. After a few minutes, she'd torn the overhanging snow down completely. With her ski boot, she kicked into the wall of snow, at the height of her knee, making a step. Then she dug other steps with her gloved hands, getting warm as she labored over her task.

It didn't work. She could get up onto the first step, but she couldn't get any grip with her hand, to hold herself against the wall and advance farther. Her ski and poles were no use as supports either. In frustration, she threw the other ski out of the opening, and then she heard a high-pitched squeal.

Tessa held her breath. It had definitely not been a human sound. She whistled.

Nothing. Had she imagined it?

No. It had to be one of them.

"Please, barbegazi. I can't get out," she called.

Although she had wished for and almost expected it, the next thing that happened surprised Tessa: six fingers and a furry head appeared at the top of the hole. Two pointed ears and a rather large potato-like nose stuck out of the shaggy whitish fur. Beneath bushy eyebrows, a pair of ice-blue, beady eyes were staring at her.

FROM *HABITS & HABITATS: A HISTORIC ACCOUNT OF ALPINE ELVES* BY PROFESSOR DR. EBERHART LUDWIG FRITZ BAHNE

According to Foubergé's 1781 written account,* barbegazi have forty-two words for snow. This number most likely included repetition of several words in a variety of French and Swiss local dialects.

Barbegazi classify snow based on wetness, smell, taste, color, season, the size of the individual crystals, and avalanche risk factor.

Their love of avalanches prompted Foubergé to adopt the collective noun "avalanche" and hence describe an "avalanche of barbegazi."

---

*Foubergé, A.S. 1781: Elves of the Central Alps. Paris: Éditions Féerique, 24–26.

9

Gawion

Gawion lay on his stomach and looked down into the hole, rubbing his arm where the wooden foot had grazed it. A numbing tingle spread from his shoulder to his fingertips. Beyond a doubt, those long pretend feet contained other materials than wood.

A human child, a baby, younger than Liel, peered up at him, without swooning or shrieking. It smiled. Had it said "barbegazi"? Was this a trap? The elf hunters of his daymares were grown and menacing, nothing like this.

He jumped up, sniffing and scanning the surroundings, but found nothing except a faint whiff of metal from the sticks in its hand and those unnatural feet.

"Help me, barbegazi! Please!" it screamed.

Good. It sounded frightened, and it was trapped. Gawion shoved his toes into the snow as anchors, lay down again, and stared at the human.

He had never observed a conscious one up close before. Two funny braided beards poked out from under the raspberry-like shell on its head. The tree-trunk-colored braids hung under its ears, not, as beards normally did, under the nose. Did these side-beards have any special function?

"Please help me," the human said. Eyes the color of ragged peaks stared up at him, while springs flowed from them and dripped onto the floor.

If Maeg was imprisoned somewhere, perhaps an exchange could take place. If he found Maeg and her abductor... Perhaps Papa could guard this human while he searched the village? But, no, that might take too long. It would catch its death in the cold. Bringing it home was no solution either—the glacier block cooled the cave, not to mention Maman's reaction.

"Please, barbegazi."

Should he help it out? No others would travel this route so late. Without an avalanche, a search party's appearance was very unlikely. The reckless creature was alone. And it had nothing to do with Maeg's disappearance, or he would have caught a trace of his sister's thawing-spring-snow scent.

The streams from the human's eyes dried up. Its mouth, unhidden by a beard or fur, formed a tilted new moon, exposing single rows of odd, square teeth. It looked so friendly.

Gawion's stomach grumbled.

"Have you brought the berry gift?" The words, spoken in the human tongue, flew out of his mouth. He wanted to stuff his whole beard down his throat to stop them.

"Berry gift? What's that?"

Oh, why had he spoken? This was not the right human. Gawion withdrew from the rim.

"Hey! Come back." The voice turned panicky again. "Please, barbegazi! I... I need your help. I won't tell anyone."

Humans were deceptive. He mistrusted it, but he had to help. That was what they did, when they found living humans buried in the snow. After marching ten paces away from the hole, he began shoveling with his enormous feet. The top layer of snow was light and fluffy powder, and the soundless digging required no effort. The cries of help behind him continued. When his claws hit a crusty layer of old snow, the scraping drowned out the screams. He took a moment to savor the chill and harvest an icy lump to suck on. Then his feet let loose again, cutting a horizontal tunnel.

Just before he broke through the thin snow wall, he paused to prepare himself. The shell on this one's fragile head troubled him, and he had not rescued anyone conscious in a long time. After considering the size of this human, he revised Papa's lessons about their anatomy and the best walloping spots.

Gawion shot out of the tunnel. Swirling in the air, he oriented himself toward it, his walloping arm outstretched.

"Tha—" The impact cut off its voice, and it sank to the ground, lifeless as an aestivating barbegazi.

Yes! Gawion pumped his fist in triumph. Now he just had to get rid of it, and prevent it from ever returning.

10

Tessa

"**H**ey, kid, wake up."

Tessa opened one eye and saw a pair of heavy brown shoes, dark green socks, and hairy legs below leather knickerbockers. She groaned.

"Take me home…" she mumbled, and hummed a few notes.

"What's that? You okay?"

With a huge effort, she rolled onto her back. A pimpled boy stood bent over her. His expression wavered between concern and irritation. A checkered shirt and a green felt vest completed his outfit. Formal wear.

"Was that you whistling?" he asked.

The back protector riding up her neck, or something under her ski helmet, blocked her from shaking her head. The goggles. They had slid down in front and almost choked her. She groaned again. Warm light shone out of a glass door onto the porch where she lay. A wreath of holly and red berries hung above gold-etched text and a row of stars. Tessa knew she recognized the door, but the letters kept slipping out of focus, and the four, or maybe five, golden stars danced. Where had the hole in the snow gone?

"You can't lie in front of the hotel entrance."

Wasn't he the big brother of someone in her class? A trainee waiter?

He glanced inside, then back at Tessa before he opened the door. Bells tinkled. "Harry! Hey, Harry!"

Her head hurt. Perhaps she'd bumped it when she tumbled into that hole. But how did she get to the village? She remembered being trapped in the snow, desperate to escape, then misty fumes, like dry-ice, surrounding her, and now she lay here as if by magic.

"Harry," the waiter called through the open door. "You know all the ski kids, right?"

Why had he asked if she whistled? The barbegazi had whistled, long before she landed in the hole. The barbegazi. She'd seen one, hadn't she? It was real, wasn't it? How else had she escaped? She closed her eyes, recalling the details. The beady eyes, set deep in the thick fur. The tangled beard snaking round one of the three-fingered hands. If only she'd seen the feet. The barbegazi had said something. Something she understood...

"Tessa!" Someone in white, with a floor-length black apron, squatted and shook her. "Are you all right? What happened?" Uncle Harry propped her up.

Her head spun. "I crashed..."

"Tell Mick to mind the mushroom soup. I'll take Tessa home. Won't be more than ten minutes."

"Yes, chef." The waiter disappeared, to the jingle of bells.

"Is Susi or Aunt Gertrude home?" Uncle Harry tugged at the goggles and pulled them up onto her helmet.

The dense fog in her brain cleared.

"Oma's always home," she said.

Where was the barbegazi? Did something move among the fir trees at the far side of the parking lot just now? Falling lumps of wet snow obstructed her view.

"What are you looking for?" Uncle Harry was following her gaze.

"The... My skis." It wasn't even a lie. Where were her skis? The poles, her new World Cup Lekis, stood in the snow below the porch.

"I can see something." Uncle Harry ran across the parking lot and came back carrying her skis, or rather, what used to be her skis. "What on earth did you do to them?"

Tessa blinked. Was she seeing double? No, both skis had been broken almost in half behind the binding. Only the metal edges held the halves together. Ragged wood splinters peeked out between the waxed black bottom and the enameled top. Her new Atomic skis, ruined.

She slumped, sliding sideways.

In a haze, Uncle Harry drove her home. Afterward, he helped Oma upstairs so she could watch Tessa until Mum came. He thought Tessa might have a concussion. Tessa thought he might be right.

She lay on the sofa all evening, dozing and humming a song that was stuck in her head, while Oma sat in the armchair with her crossword puzzle. Every time Tessa fell asleep, Oma woke her, like you're supposed to with concussions, just in case.

"I should be taking care of you," Tessa mumbled, but Oma just smiled and fetched water and cool cloths. Perhaps she was better at fussing over someone than being made a fuss of.

"The barbegazi must've carried me," Tessa said, when she began to feel less woozy, and asked if Oma believed she'd seen one.

"Of course, dear," Oma replied.

But would anyone else? They hadn't believed Opa. Not even Mum, who'd been away at hotelier school at the time. "Why didn't Opa care that no one believed him?"

Oma shrugged. "He'd have been just as skeptical if he hadn't seen the barbegazi with his own eyes."

Later, Mum rushed in the door, calling, "How is she? How are you, Mum? Are you both okay?"

She ran to the sofa, seizing Tessa, saying how sorry she was, how she would've come earlier—the restaurant wasn't even busy—but she'd forgotten her phone in the car and only seen Harry's message when she was on her way home.

"My darling girl," Mum said, over and over again. Her fussing was frantic compared to Oma's, but Tessa leaned into the hard embrace.

Oma and Mum whispered for a long time in the hallway before Mum helped Oma downstairs.

"Could I have some hot chocolate, Mum?" Tessa sat up, discarding the wool blanket. The song in her head had stopped and the red digits on the oven, *11:41*, didn't wiggle any more. Everything seemed normal, except her journey from the snow, which remained a blur. And, of course, the barbegazi.

Mum brought her a steaming cup with a thick layer of whipped cream on top. She still wore her ankle-length *dirndl* costume—the waitress uniform—and she sat at the other end of the sofa, kneading her temples, without speaking for a while.

"So you fell into a hole in Schöngraben, got rescued by a fairy who delivered you to Hotel Lawinenfang, but ruined your brand new skis. That about right?" Mum finally said, in a matter-of-fact tone.

Tessa stirred her drink and nodded. "Barbegazi are actually not fairies—"

"I don't know where to start, Tessa..." Mum snatched the blanket from the floor and began folding it. "This obsession of yours has to stop. In what fantasy world would you ever be allowed to ski through Schöngraben alone? If that's what you did. And how could you ruin your skis? Your father sent money for those, and you know I can't afford—" She scrunched the blanket into a ball and threw it back onto the floor. "Perhaps I shouldn't let you ski at all, if you can't keep even the simplest rules. You never ski off-piste alone. Never."

Mum's voice had changed from shrill to choked, and she leaned forward, placing her face in her hands.

"I'm sorry," Tessa mumbled. "I didn't mean to—"

"Promise me..." Mum straightened and turned to look Tessa in the eyes. "I want you to promise to never ski off-piste without adult supervision again."

Tessa hesitated. She had found a barbegazi. It wasn't something she'd imagined. But how would she ever find it again without skiing off-piste on her own?

In a tiny voice, she said, "I promise."

11

Gawion

Gawion drew a breath of relief. The tall human who had fetched the broken wooden feet had looked so much like the berry-human that he had almost shown himself. At the last moment, he wondered at its lack of beard and noticed how it resembled the berry-human of decades ago, not the berry-human he had seen last winter.

The two humans disappeared in a vehicle, with a loud roar. All human mechanical inventions polluted the mountain silence: the wheeled vehicles, the contraptions for transporting humans up the snow-covered slopes, and, worst of all, the flying vehicles topped with rotating metal blades.

Sometimes, after avalanches, those machines flew above Schöngraben, close to the cave, making a whirlwind of powder snow. They scared Gawion. Maeg too, although she liked it when they dropped explosive devices to blast snow cornices and release avalanches. The loud bangs scared him even more, though he had not told Maeg. Life had been easier when the humans used horses and carts, and stayed away from the high mountains.

Gawion had not been so close to the village in decades, and he stared transfixed at the imposing human dwelling, while he inched backward through the rows of fir trees. Nearby, dogs bayed.

Another vehicle arrived. Its light beams lit up the trees and millions of snowflakes. Gawion froze, standing immobile as a glacier. Two majestic firs cast long shadows beside him, but only a sapling grew between him and the vehicle. A dog barked somewhere. Turn off the lights, he prayed. Doors slammed, and human voices moved away. The lights still shone.

"You forgot the headlights again," a deep voice said.

One human returned to the vehicle. It stared right at him and said, "What *is* that?"

"Rrroowff! Rrroowff!" In one fluid motion, Gawion turned, got down on all fours, pretending to be a dog, barked and bolted. He kicked and shoved with his legs, sweeping piles of snow over the imprints of his long feet.

Howls and baying answered him, but he did not stop until pine branches slapped against him, blurring his vision, in the forest.

"Rooooowf," a bark greeted him from not far behind. It translated into: "What's up, mate?" and a large dog slunk toward him.

Gawion panted, trying to catch his breath. He wanted to hide—dogs were as bad as humans—but he could not run any more. His own barks had been a survival instinct, born by the background noise of baying dogs. He realized now that he had barked, "Help. The humans are after me." Or something like that. He was uncertain of the local dialect, and, though elves spoke all languages, Dog was a whole new snowball game. Intonation played a key role. Meaning changed depending on where in the throat the sounds were initiated. Barbegazi necks are nearly invisible, so Gawion had little to work with. As did many dog breeds. Not this one though. Its long, broad neck rippled with thick folds of short-haired, tree-trunk-colored fur.

"You okay?" the dog asked.

"Yes, thank you."

"Rraaooooo." The dog howled from deep in its throat. "Situation under control. Relax," rang out across the valley.

A chorus of distant yaps answered.

"Call me Brownie," the dog barked. It sat next to Gawion, stuck its pink tongue out and panted.

"Gawion."

"Are you one of those fancy dog types? I'm a Labrador myself." Brownie studied him with kind, starless-night eyes. They were glazed over, and Gawion got the distinct feeling Brownie's eyesight was poor. "Haven't seen anyone quite like you before." The neck stretched, growing even longer. A wet nose nuzzled him. Brownie sniffed. "Hmmm. Your scent is odd."

The wet dog stench overpowered Gawion, who leaned away. He only knew the names of two dog types: Rottweilers and bloodhounds. The dogs that hunted innocent creatures. Maman's recollections of those horrifying monsters, chasing them as they escaped the zoological garden at Schönbrunn, gave him daymares, and he hoped he would never meet either.

"Have you no humans?" he asked, to distract Brownie. The village dogs he had seen from a distance were tied up or fenced in by their humans.

"Yeah, but I'm a free spirit. I go home when I need food and a warm hearth."

Gawion sighed. He longed for the morning, when he might curl up in front of the ice cooler. His sigh must have meant more in Dog, because Brownie turned his half-blind eyes toward him again, and said, "What's the problem, mate?"

"I fear humans have abducted my sister. I am searching for her."

"Does she smell anything like you?" Brownie snuffled again.

"I suppose so." Gawion did not know how to describe that sweet scent of thawing spring snow, in any language except his own.

"I'll have a sniff around. Ask my mates."

"Thanks."

"Meet you here tomorrow night," Brownie barked, and he padded off back toward the village.

No matter what Maman said about dogs, Gawion was not afraid of this creature. Perhaps he had even found a friend in the village. Someone he could trust.

He lifted his beard and sniffed where Brownie's nose had nuzzled him. Yuck! After rubbing it clean and rolling in the snow, he still stank of wet dog. If he did not get rid of the odor before morning, he would be in an avalanche of trouble.

FROM *HABITS & HABITATS: A HISTORIC ACCOUNT OF ALPINE ELVES* BY PROFESSOR DR. EBERHART LUDWIG FRITZ BAHNE

Hardly any information exists about the barbegazi's diet, but snow and ice doubtless feature high on their dietary plan.

However, when captured barbegazi were given ice cubes, it rarely sustained them for more than a few weeks. Experiments with feeding them moss, pine needles, and cooked or raw alpine meats were equally unsuccessful in keeping the barbegazi alive.

WEDNESDAY, DECEMBER 28

—12—

Tessa

Tessa dreamt about skiing and snow and barbegazi, waking often to untangle her sheets. Once, she woke with a pounding heart and vivid dream images.

In the dream, she had skied through a hole into an upside-down world, where loud music blasted from invisible speakers. A giant furry creature had taken her skis and bent them into circles. "Round as a berry," it said, and smacked its unseen lips. Then it shrank—or she grew—and the creature, now clearly a barbegazi, said, "Have a blueberry, Tessa." It threw a turquoise berry the size of a watermelon toward her. Tessa opened her mouth, which expanded, to catch the berry. When she swallowed, the world spun again, the music stopped, and she stood in the hole in Schöngraben, looking up at the barbegazi. It said, "Have you brought the berry gift?"

The berry gift. That's what the barbegazi had said. She remembered now.

The wooden beams of the roof creaked. She tried to imagine

herself back in the hole, the barbegazi above her, instead of the ceiling, asking, "Have you brought the berry gift?" The words had been spoken in a clear, high-pitched voice. Definitely real, she thought, before she slipped into another dream.

When Tessa woke, bright winter light shone through a gap in the curtains. Mum had let her sleep in. The ski club would be training now. She wished she were there, racing, cold air prickling her skin. Then she remembered her ruined skis and pulled the duvet over her head, shutting out the light.

The berry gift! She jumped out of bed and grabbed the black book on top of her piled-up school books. Opening it, she flipped to the barbegazi chapter and skimmed the pages. The book contained interesting information about barbegazi fur and feet and iron cages, but no references to berries or gifts.

While she ate a late breakfast, she mulled over the mysterious berry gift. Mum was at home, folding laundry. She scolded Tessa for skiing off-piste alone, and nagged her about remembering to "live in the real world." Tessa only half-listened and nodded whenever Mum paused.

"Oma's dusting her cupboards and bookcases this afternoon," Mum said. "I offered to do it, now that I'm taking the day off anyway, but she wants to do it herself."

Tessa looked up. "That's good, right?"

Mum shrugged. "I just hope it's not too much for her. Perhaps she'll let you help."

"Okay," Tessa said. "She can't do the top shelves herself."

She didn't need to add that Opa used to do those—Mum's eyes became glassy before she turned away, nodding.

Later, standing on the ladder, she wiped dust from Opa's trophies. On the biggest, a prize from the Austrian downhill championships more than forty years ago, an inset of shiny, red crystals—Tessa used to think they were rubies—sparkled like redcurrants after rain. Her thoughts wandered to the barbegazi dream.

Oma swept the duster over the grandfather clock. She appeared to have even more energy than last night. It seemed safe to ask.

"Did Opa ever mention a berry gift?"

"Him and his berries. The freezer's so full of berries, I could hardly find room for the Tupperware of leftover goulash soup." Oma dusted the long pendulum of the clock, and it skipped a few beats. "For years I suspected he gave them to Mrs. Huber. The Hubers never had much, and after she was widowed... She was his childhood sweetheart, you know."

In a flash, Tessa thought of old Mrs. Huber—brandishing her walking stick, her mouth tugged down in a constant look of disapproval.

Sniffing, Oma pulled an embroidered handkerchief out of her sleeve. After drying her eyes, she muttered, "I didn't speak to her for decades."

"But he gave them to the barbegazi?"

"Of course he did. And to his very last moment he spoke about it. 'Remember the berries on the twenty-first of December' he said, 'Remember to tell Tessa—'" Oma let her hand with the duster fall. "What date is it, dear?"

"It's after Christmas."

"Oh, Ohhhh…" Oma drew the sigh out. Like a balloon leaking air, she deflated and sank into the squishy armchair.

Alarmed, Tessa jumped down from the ladder.

Oma's face had turned quite white. Tiny beads of sweat appeared on her forehead. "I promised him," she whispered, clutching her chest, her breathing becoming ragged.

"Oma! Shall I get Mum? Your pills? Call the doctor?"

"Fe-fetch. Su-Susi. Pills," Oma stuttered, and Tessa ran up the stairs, calling for her mother.

Tessa helped Mum get Oma wrapped in her coat and out into the car. Before she closed the passenger door, she hugged Oma and whispered in her ear, "Don't worry. I'll bring the berries to the barbegazi," but she wasn't sure Oma heard.

13

Gawion

The moment Gawion slid into the cave, on his belly, he regretted coming home. Maman screeched, Papa bellowed his name, and Liel, scared of the noise, wailed, her nose turning glacier-blue. Papa whistled one of those whistles that is audible ten kilometers away in the right wind conditions. Gawion rose, edging back, until he stood against the snow wall.

"THE VILLAGE!" Papa bellowed. "HAVE I NOT TOLD YOU"—he paused to inhale—"under no circumstances, to get within a hundred barbegazi feet of the human dwellings?"

Gawion opened his mouth to speak, but Maman beat him to it.

"How could you? We are already worried sick about Maeg."

"But—"

"What is this?" Maman sniffed, then she pushed Papa aside—no mean feat—and strode toward Gawion. He forced himself not to duck. She snuffled with her large nose. "Your stench. That is not dog, is it?"

"DOG?" In one leap, Papa had landed on his other side, thrusting his boulder of a nose into Gawion's beard. Both of them sniffed at him as if they were dogs themselves, reminding him of Brownie. Gawion pressed his lips together to stop an improper urge to laugh.

"For the love of snow, tell me you have not been consorting with dogs." Maman spoke softly, her tone pleading. It wiped his sense of amusement away. He would have preferred it if she had screeched.

"A very friendly dog," he muttered.

With their long feet, his parents blocked him from moving, and their fur stood on end, tingling. He could sense them exchanging glances above his head.

"Oh, Gawion." Maman sighed. "Never trust a dog. They do the bidding of humans."

"Your maman believed the imperial dogs were her friends, in Vienna. Do you remember, *ma chérie?*"

"I shall never forget." In a gentle gesture, Maman twirled strands of Papa's beard around her fingers. "Those snarling, baying beasts, tracking us to the station, despite the snowstorm—"

"If the train had not departed right after we got Grandpère up on its roof, we would still be stuck in that iron cage as part of the imperial menagerie."

Keep talking, Gawion thought. The longer they talked, the calmer they became. Perhaps they would forget all about him.

"Yuck, yuckety-yuck. Why does Gawion smell so bad?" Liel,

her nose a normal snow-color again, had sneaked past her parents and now stood underneath Gawion's chin.

Papa swiveled on the spot. "Yes. Explain yourself."

Gawion took a deep breath, his brain whirling, trying to find a way to avoid being grounded and having to watch Liel while Maman searched with Papa.

He told them the whole story, from finding the human, who seemed to know what he was, in the hole, to his meeting with Brownie. Or, almost the whole story.

When Gawion explained how he had transported the human and her broken wooden feet to a big dwelling on the edge of the village, Papa tensed and said, "You moved into their artificial light? You could have been seen," and grasped his hand. "Good thinking, posing as a dog."

Gawion did not mention that he only pretended to be a dog after he was in fact seen.

Maman shook her head while he talked, mumbling "Never trust a dog" over and over. So he neglected to inform them of his meeting with Brownie tonight.

They did not ground him, but he had also not mentioned the worst thing. His biggest mistake. The crucial part missing from his explanation. The one thing he omitted, after careful consideration: that he had spoken to the human.

14

Tessa

Back in Oma's kitchen, Tessa crouched to open the freezer. The drawers stuck, filled to the rim with berries in clear plastic bags. Oma usually wrote content and date and weight on frozen food. Nothing marked these bags—another sign they were meant for the barbegazi. But how could she deliver them without skiing off-piste?

Tessa wished she'd not been left at home. The ticks from the grandfather clock amplified the emptiness of the room. "Just go on ticking," she muttered, and ran upstairs.

She turned on the TV, flipping through reruns and cartoons, until she let the weather channel fill the house with sound and flickering light. After retrieving her phone from the charger, she curled up on the sofa, waiting for Mum and Oma to return.

Felix had sent three messages. The first read: u r as crazy as ur opa. The second, an animation of a stick figure snapping her skis in half, made her smile. And the third was good news:

come by tmrw b4 ski to fit my old skis 4u. Only 2 x training until race! At least she could get up on the slopes tomorrow.

Returning to the elf book, she studied the barbegazi chapter again, and read snippets about limestone-cave goblins and mountain-spring sprites.

Later, Mum sent a message: Oma okay. Am driving her to hospital for tests. Go to Lisa's or there's soup in the fridge. Mum xxx.

If they were going to the hospital, it didn't sound as if Oma was okay.

The cozy kitchen and the homemade desserts at Lisa's tempted Tessa. But Maria would be there, or Lisa would be at Maria's. They'd bragged about their daily sleepovers. She didn't really mind leftover soup, and she wasn't even hungry.

But the barbegazi she'd seen might be hungry, craving the berries Opa used to bring. And if barbegazi ate berries, then she knew something that professor didn't. He'd be so grateful when she told him, he'd definitely mention her in his next book!

Opa had wanted Oma to tell her about the berries… Tessa bit her lip. Perhaps there was another way of reaching the barbegazi hole. She'd promised Mum not to ski off-piste alone. She hadn't promised not to go hiking alone. The nearest hospital was thirty kilometers away. Would that give her enough time?

As a precaution, she wrote two notes. The first, *I'm going over to Lisa's*, she fixed to the fridge with the Merlion magnet Dad had sent from Singapore. She placed the second on her pillow, where Mum wouldn't look unless she became worried.

In scrawling letters she'd written: *If Lisa's not home, I'll walk up to Schöngraben.*

After pulling on thermal long johns and thick, striped socks, she rummaged in the attic until she found Mum's big rucksack—the one they used for overnight hikes in summer. Downstairs, she lined the rucksack with a heavy-duty blue plastic carrier bag, and filled it with the frozen berries. Less than half of them fitted inside, but going upstairs she swayed under the rucksack's weight. With her outdoor clothes on, she trudged outside and into the garage. Her ruined skis lay by the trash meant for the garbage station. She shuddered. Breaking alpine skis required immense force. She'd always thought of the barbegazi as cuddly creatures. Perhaps they weren't quite as harmless as she'd imagined.

Although she searched, she couldn't find her snowshoes. Last season, after the final race, when ski training stopped, she'd often used them with Lisa. They would walk up the slopes, chatting, and sit on a bench in the sun, before running downward, sliding through powder snow up to their knees. They always exited the forest on Jakobsweg, the old pilgrimage route through Europe which led all the way to Santiago de Compostela in Spain, then half-glided to Lisa's house, and drank hot chocolate in that cozy kitchen. The snowshoes were probably still at Lisa's.

Opa's snowshoes hung on the wall, above her broken skis. They looked like relics from the Stone Age. The wood, bent into the shape of elongated tennis rackets, gleamed. As usual, Opa had oiled them in the spring. The strings and the smooth leather straps seemed new, yet they had been old long before

Tessa was born. They weighed a lot compared to her own high-tech aluminum snowshoes, but they were better than nothing. She strapped them onto the sides of the rucksack, and borrowed Mum's lightweight, adjustable hiking poles.

On her way through the darkening village, a ski bus rumbled past, its snow chains grinding on the gravel. A group of wobbly ski-boot walkers shouted après-ski song refrains. To avoid them, Tessa crossed the road. Behind the last houses, the road became a steep track. Sweat ran down her brow under the knitted hat. She huffed, and her shoulders ached.

Two sleds rushed toward her, their riders squealing and laughing. Tessa shrieked and jumped sideways to escape being hit. The toboggan run was open tonight, even though it was Wednesday—above her, on the track leading up the mountain, splotches of warm yellow light gleamed among the snow-covered trees.

Another group of tobogganists sped past. Tessa crept along the edge of the track until she crossed the bridge over the mountain stream and the sharp turn-off to the toboggan run. From here on, there would be no more sleds and no more light.

By the last lamp post, she secured her headlamp and tightened the leather straps of the snowshoes round her boots. When she was done, her breathing had slowed. She shivered and took a few tentative steps. Although she walked with her feet wide apart, the heavy things still clanged together. Her legs were too short to heave Opa's snowshoes far enough to lift their wobbly back ends. Should she take them off again and just walk on the hardened ski trails? No. If she accidentally stepped off those tracks, she might sink into soft snow.

"No falling into holes today." She trudged forward, finding a slow rhythm. Pole in, lift opposite foot, drag forward, set down, pole in, lift, drag...

The two huge mounds, which marked the entrance to Schöngraben, and protected the village from avalanches, loomed above her. When she passed between them, the faint shrieks from the toboggan run died away.

On skis, the lower part of the gorge seemed flat, but it was steeper than most roads, and soon her whole body ached. Her shins cramped. She whistled—not a tune, just individual hoarse tones—but she lacked air. The thumping blood in her ears, and her ragged breathing, made it difficult to hear if anyone whistled in answer.

From up near the trees, on her right, came a faint swishing sound. There couldn't be tobogganists here. Or skiers, so late. Could it be a barbegazi?

Tessa stopped and turned. Her headlamp drew a dark green circle on the black forest. "Hel-lo," she called, her voice cracking. "Anybody there?"

Silence.

She continued her slow ascent, whistling and calling, "Hello bar-be-gaziii... I'm bringing the berry gift."

15

Gawion

In the cave, the day had felt endless. Maman recited her terrifying dog-tales and kept repeating her "never trust a dog" mantra. Despite her scrubbing his beard with all kinds of snow, Gawion still stank. That set both her and Papa off whenever he neared their wrinkled noses. If it had not, he might have confessed and told them he had spoken to the human.

But what did it matter? He had only asked about the berry gift, and, after his memory charm, the human would have forgotten ever seeing him.

What he would not give for the berry gift! The blackberry he had shared with Liel helped less in his hollow stomach than a snowflake trying to fill the crack in a glacier.

Outside in the pleasant evening gloom, they prepared to resume the search. Papa pointed him to the bare rocks above the tree line. The least likely place to find Maeg.

"We should search below the avalanche, Papa."

"Have you not already trawled the area from the avalanche

to the earth mounds? Or did you neglect your duties, in your haste to go on adventures in the village?"

"I did not," Gawion answered, feeling blood pound all the way up to the points of his ears. Every snowflake of the scar left by the avalanche had been combed. And every boulder and lump of snow below had been turned during that first frantic night. Twice. First with Papa, and then again on his own. "How about beyond Schöngraben? In the village."

"Too dangerous. If Maeg has indeed been taken, she might be used as bait to lure us thither. That is how they captured Maman and Grandpère, when they tried to rescue me."

"I know, I know." Gawion stopped Papa before he got into his storytelling stride. He had heard about those particular events hundreds of times. They were a chapter of the cautionary tales told to keep him and Maeg away from humans. "But we could sneak around the village, listen to the dogs. They might reveal news of Maeg."

Papa rubbed his chin under its long beard, and sighed.

Gawion, sensing his uncertainty, pressed on. "She is not lying under the snow, Papa. She has been taken. It was your first instinct when we found the fur."

Papa stood with hunched shoulders, staring down at the village—his fear both obvious and contagious.

Dots of light littered the darkening valley, creeping up toward the surrounding night forests. From up here, where few trees grew, the lights seemed as distant and mysterious as the emerging stars.

After a long time, Papa said, "All right. I will go to the village. You must stay in Schöngraben."

"But, Papa—"

"There will be no discussion. Search the bottom part again, if you must, but do not cross between the human-made earth mounds. Understood?"

Gawion nodded. Brownie would have to come into Schöngraben.

Near the bottom of the gorge, they parted. Papa continued, hidden by the trees. Gawion passed the hole where he had found the human just yesterday. Its gaping emptiness neither surprised nor disappointed him. His stomach reacted, though, with a faint grumble.

He followed the mountain stream—the only area with no human tracks—stopping at intervals to kick at mounds in the snow. He had already searched here. If only he had been able to persuade Papa to let him go to the village!

He heard a feeble human whistle, coming from a strange light cone farther down the narrow valley. A voice called, "Berry gift."

Gawion sniffed. No, that could not be. His stomach growled in response. A smile spread below his beard. Finally, the berry-human had come. Excited, he surfed toward the light, careful to stay clear of its beam.

"Berry gift," the human called again. It stopped. The light was shining out from its head. The human dimmed the brightness until it cast an oval pale shape on the snow.

With a jolt, Gawion recognized the human he had found in

the hole yesterday. How could it come back, when he had ruined its wooden feet? And how could it remember? His charm should have filled its head with that horrible noise.

The usual winter forest stillness seeped out from the shadows under the trees. Underneath the berry aroma, the air carried only the faintest tang of iron.

The human dumped a large pack on the ground, fumbled inside it, and extracted a see-through bag. Even from this distance, Gawion could see the small blood-colored balls, and hear the dull clicks they made when the human shook the bag. It used its teeth to tear the transparent material. The delicious scent of raspberries engulfed Gawion. His stomach rumbled and the human looked up, pointing the light beam to a place just in front of his toes.

It threw a handful of berries out beyond the light. Gawion hurried to sniff them out. The first four he swallowed without taking time to enjoy them. He had to stay alert. The rest he collected and dropped into the little pocket Maman had knotted in the middle of his beard. He would save them for her.

The human threw more berries, but this time they landed inside the light. One of them was just at the edge though. He might be able to snatch it, without the human noticing. Then again... The human stood completely still, probably staring at exactly that berry.

"I've brought the berry gift," it said.

Gawion could not leave without all those berries. Perhaps if he walloped the human and took them... But that was an impolite response to someone bringing food, and then it most certainly would not bring any more.

The light cone moved to the side. Now was his chance. His arm shot out and seized the berry, but the light returned too soon.

"I'm not going to harm you," it said. The human poured berries into the snow by its feet, dotting the ground with blood-colored spots. "The berries are from my grandfather."

Was this really a descendent of the berry-human? He sniffed, inhaling deep through his large nose, but the sweet berries over-powered any particulars of the human's scent. He supposed it could be true. Why else would it bring berries?

"He broke his leg in an avalanche right up there, years and years ago." The human pointed. "One of you saved him and helped him home."

That *was* true. Gawion only hesitated for a moment more before he said, "To be sure, it was I."

16

Tessa

In two leaps and a flurry of white powder, the barbegazi landed next to Tessa. Up close he—or she—looked even stranger than in Opa's sketched drawings. Like an upright, cuddly teddy-polar-bear, with the biggest feet she'd ever seen. She wanted to sing and dance and jump around, but, fearful of frightening it, she stood without moving while the barbegazi snatched the berries at her feet.

Most of them disappeared into a parting in the middle of its long beard, but it scooped one three-fingered handful of snow and berries into its mouth, and gulped down the mixture with loud smacks. Talk about craving berries. It must've been starving.

The barbegazi only reached her shoulder, and hedgerow-like eyebrows hid its eyes, so she tried to get down on her knees to look into its face. Her snowshoes clanked together. The barbegazi swirled its head toward them, then up at Tessa, like a startled animal. It stopped chewing and stared at her. Instead of trying to get down on her knees, Tessa slowly leaned back until she was half-sitting on the sturdy frame of the rucksack. She adjusted the beam of her headlamp, so it didn't shine directly on the barbegazi. The creature's ice-blue eyes followed her movements.

"I'm Tessa. What's your name?" Inside the mitten, she crossed her fingers, willing it to speak.

"Gawion." He bent his head in a formal bow. The gesture, worthy of a ballroom filled with royalty, was at odds with the yellowish, gleaming fur, which hung in clumps encrusted with ice.

Tessa gave a quick nod. How could she get it to talk?

Before she thought of a question, Gawion asked, "Where is your grandfather?"

The pitch of his voice—for she was certain it was a he, now—reminded her of those "Staying Alive" singers Mum liked, or someone speaking after inhaling from a helium balloon, but without the mirth.

"He died. Twenty-eight days ago." The familiar lump grew in her throat. This, the barbegazi, was what Opa had planned to show her. They should've been here together, and then told Oma all about it afterward. She blinked to keep the tears at bay.

"Allow me to condole." Gawion bent his head. "That explains the missing berry gift."

"Did you help me out of the hole yesterday?"

A third bow, before he rubbed his belly, streaking his beard with red spirals.

"I apologize for the damage to your wooden feet."

Tessa shuddered. Not because she was scared, but because Gawion's bow sent an icy breeze toward her. It was as if he were radiating coldness. Despite the state of her skis, she wasn't scared at all.

"Why'd you break them?"

"I presumed it would prevent your return. Obviously, I was mistaken."

Tessa smiled.

"I wanted to find one of you. And I did. Now they have to believe me." She could even take a photo and send it to that professor. The whole world would know the barbegazi weren't extinct! "Will you come with me? So my friends can see you?"

The ice-blue eyes gazed deep into Tessa's, then Gawion shook his head, the long beard swinging from side to side.

"Please. You must come. I brought berries," she said. "I have more berries at home. You can have all of them."

He sighed. At least, it sounded like a sigh.

"Please. No one believes me. Everyone says you're extinct."

"It is better that way."

Hot tears welled up in her eyes. The barbegazi blurred around the edges.

"But why?" she asked with a sob.

"Your sort will want to capture us."

"My friends wouldn't do that," Tessa said. But others might, she knew. In school, they'd just finished their endangered species project, where they'd learned about gorillas and pandas and snow leopards, and breeding programs in captivity. In that light, some of the entries in the elf book took on a new meaning. Perhaps she shouldn't tell that professor she'd found a barbegazi.

"That's why Opa lied," she said. "He lied to protect you." Or maybe the professor lied in his book, to protect the barbegazi? Opa had never stopped talking about his rescuer, and the whole village had mocked him for it. The puzzle baffled her, but clearly someone had made an effort to keep the barbegazi's existence secret.

"Okay. I won't tell anyone about you," she promised. "And don't worry, no one even suspects you're still around."

"I fear that is not entirely true," Gawion said. "You see, my sister has been missing since the big avalanche." He nodded up toward the Törli couloir.

"Let me fetch a shovel and help you search," Tessa offered.

"You are most kind, but Maeg—Maegorodiel—is not here. Not under the snow. It is much worse."

"What's worse than being buried under the snow?"

"Being held captive in the village."

"But who?..." Few people had skied off-piste on Monday, when the avalanche warning was so high. On Kapall, she'd only seen the man in white. Then she remembered the whistling guest at Felix's house.

"It might be nothing," she told Gawion, "but I have an idea."

FROM *HABITS & HABITATS: A HISTORIC ACCOUNT OF ALPINE ELVES* BY PROFESSOR DR. EBERHART LUDWIG FRITZ BAHNE

Barbegazi aestivate, spending the months from May to October in a deep sleep, below one of Europe's ever-shrinking glaciers. Global warming and re-treating glaciers* are therefore believed to be major contributing factors in their presumed extinction.

Statistically, the best time to capture barbegazi is in October. In several documented cases from Mer de Glace in France and Great Aletsch Glacier in Switzerland, the creatures have stumbled sleepily out of their dens, into traps set in glacier crevasses.

---

*Measured retreat of the Great Aletsch Glacier (the largest glacier in Switzerland) from 1870 to 1990 amounts to two kilometers, or close to ten percent of its length. Since 1980, glaciers around the world have been losing mass at an accelerated rate.

17

Gawion

"Let me help you with the berries first." The human, Tessa, got up. It was taller than Papa. As it tilted the big pack toward him, he saw the countless see-through bags, filled with berries, inside. Berries and more berries. Perhaps enough to feed them until the summer sleep.

"D'you want more raspberries?"

Gawion licked his lips. "Please." With so many berries, he could eat a few more without feeling bad.

Tessa smiled and poured raspberries into his cupped hand, spilling several, which Gawion snatched up from the snow. He scooped them into his mouth and closed his eyes, savoring the cold lumps.

"Good?"

He opened his eyes and nodded, trying to say "delicious," but only managed a grunt. His mouth had not been full of berries since he woke in the autumn. Maman, as usual, had risen days before the rest of them. She had gathered a whole mountain of berries, and her beard, which she knotted into a basket, was striped in colors of a sunset sky. As always, just after aestivation, Gawion had been allowed to eat as many berries as he wanted, and, starved as he was, he had eaten five whole handfuls.

Later in the year, they scraped snow away from brambles and found half-ripe and half-rotten berries underneath. Tessa's berries were much better, because they had been picked just when they were ripe. The raspberries dissolved in his mouth, and the tasty juice filled him with pleasure and energy. His belly gave a slow, satisfied growl.

Tessa made odd noises, like a small bird hiccupping. "You look like a vampire with blood running down your chin."

He finished chewing and gave the sort of courteous bow Maman had taught him to. "I am much obliged to you." He did not want to reveal that he had no clue what a vampire was. Probably some type of dog. Dog! He was supposed to be meeting the dog.

"Excuse me a moment," he said. Then he bayed, "Brownie?"

A distant howl answered with something he did not quite catch, perhaps about Brownie sniffing him out.

"What was that?" Tessa had begun to jump and do strange things with its arms. Almost as if it thought it could fly. Perhaps this human was a little bit peculiar.

"A prior engagement. Are you attempting to... to take to the skies?"

"You're so funny. That's not in the book." Tessa bird-hiccupped again and stopped moving its arms and legs. "I'm freezing cold."

"Aha. And you do not like that?"

"No. D'you want to borrow the rucksack to carry the berries?" Tessa lifted the blood-colored pack with all the scary metal buckles. "It might be too big."

In stupefied shock, he saw how Tessa was swinging the thing toward him. A buckle struck the back of his arm. Gawion jerked away. Numbness spread up to his shoulder and down into his hand. Warm sweat broke out under his fur, and he felt momentarily dizzy.

"Oh, sorry. Did I hit you?" Tessa put the pack on the ground and fumbled inside. He did not think it had noticed how much the tiny amount of iron in the shiny metal had affected him.

"It is okay." He gasped.

"It's way too big for you. I can tie this with a rope, then you can pull the carrier bag." Tessa lifted out a sky-blue carrier with all the berries in it, and tied a short rope through the sun-colored handles. "Should be able to hold. I've used one of these to carry ski boots."

Gawion saw to his relief that there was no metal anywhere on the carrier.

"What's up, mate?" The big dog padded into the circle of light.

"Brownie!" Tessa patted the head of the dog and rubbed behind his floppy ears.

Brownie gave his usual greeting: "Rooooowf."

"Good dog," Tessa said and rubbed harder.

"Nice, but stupid," Brownie barked to Gawion. "Why do they always say 'good dog' when I ask them how they're doing?"

Gawion made the kind of low growl that is the same as a shrug in Dog, before he barked, "Have you found my sister?"

"I might have a trace." Brownie leaned against Tessa's legs. It had stopped rubbing him and was staring at Gawion with an open mouth.

"You understand each other?" The human looked back and forth between him and the dog.

He nodded. "And Brownie understands every word you say."

"He does?" Tessa crouched and looked into the dog's starless-night eyes. "You do?"

Brownie replied with a short bark.

"I wish I could tell someone about this, but they wouldn't believe any of it." Two shrill beeps sounded, and Tessa looked at a small, square, metal thing. "Oh, gosh. Mum's on her way home. I'm sorry. I have to go."

It fastened the pack's metal buckles round its middle. A hot shiver ran down Gawion's back, and he instinctively hugged his own stomach.

"Can we meet tomorrow night?" Tessa asked. "Closer to the village?"

"By the big earth mounds?"

Tessa frowned, then, apparently realizing what he meant, nodded.

"When?"

Gawion thought for a moment. He would prefer to split up from Papa, before he met with the human.

"When the moon is above the last mountain in the east, on this side of the valley," he said.

"D'you mean Eisenspitze?"

Gawion stiffened at the name, which meant "Iron Peak," and he could barely nod. He had forgotten that there used to be iron mines on that mountain.

Tessa turned and walked away, the strange wooden feet clanking.

"What trace?" Gawion barked.

"At a tree, by the stream on the path toward St. Jakob. I got a whiff of something there that smells like you do."

Could Maeg be there? Could the water have carried her outside Schöngraben? No. The surface was frozen and covered with snow. But whatever it was, he had to find out as much as possible. Even if it meant sneaking out of the gorge.

Brownie sat with his tongue out, panting.

Gawion ought to get the berries home. But not yet. He shoveled with his feet, hiding the sack of berries under a mound of snow. "Can you show me the place?"

Brownie growled, "Sure," and Gawion followed the lumbering dog, leaving Schöngraben.

18

Tessa

As she ran home, Opa's snowshoes, fastened to the sides of the big rucksack, swung against Tessa's arms and hips, clanking noisily over her heavy breathing. But that didn't matter. The barbegazi weren't extinct, and she had talked to one of them. Gawion.

"Gawion," she said aloud.

The name rolled off her tongue, sounding fancy and French. And Gawion needed her help. Tessa's imagination raced ahead.

Together they'd find Gawion's sister. In the future, Tessa would bring berries every year. All the barbegazi would become her friends. Scores of barbegazi babies would dance around her while she fed them raspberries. Oma would be so glad she was carrying on for Opa.

She'd become a famous barbegazi protector... No, not famous. She'd become a *secret* barbegazi protector. And she wouldn't tell anyone but Oma about them—not even Mum—until the time came to hand over the responsibility of delivering berries to her successor. Perhaps her own granddaughter. She saw herself as an old lady with long white braids, skiing ahead of a teenage girl.

At the sight of the dark house and the empty driveway, she slowed. If she wanted to keep the barbegazi a secret, then she had to start right now, by avoiding questions from Mum. Better let her think she'd been home all day.

She cast a glance at the sky. Stars twinkled. There were no heavy clouds. Good. Then Mum would park outside. The crescent moon was still far from Eisenspitze, and it was already after eight o'clock. She'd probably be meeting Gawion around nine tomorrow night, then. She giggled. Agreeing on meeting times with someone who didn't own a watch was a bit tricky, but it was all part of being a secret barbegazi protector.

After she dumped the rucksack with the snowshoes in the garage, she dashed into the house. She hid her hiking boots in the far corner under the entryway bench, and hung her damp ski clothes below several coats. Turning on all the light switches she passed, and pulling off layers, she raced through the kitchen, snatching up the note, and into her room.

When she heard the car, she stuffed her fleece and socks and the crumpled-up notes into the drawer under her bed.

"Tessa. I'm home," Mum called.

Panicked, Tessa grabbed a book from the pile on her desk and jumped into bed, pulling the sleeves of her thermal top up to her elbows and the covers up to her nose.

"Tes-saaa..." Mum drew her name out into a sigh as she

entered the room. "I've told you a million times to turn off the lights."

"Sorry," she mumbled. "Where's Oma?"

Mum sank down on the edge of the bed and hugged Tessa, long and hard. When she let go, she frowned. "Why are you wearing thermals in bed?"

"I was cold." Technically, that wasn't a lie.

Mum touched her forehead and ran a hand down to the back of her neck. "You're all sweaty. Please don't tell me you're coming down with something."

"I'm fine, Mum."

Mum stared at the book. "Learning math? During the Christmas holidays? You must be ill." She went to the dresser and pulled out a dry T-shirt and some leggings. Hugging the clothes to her chest, she just stood there like she'd forgotten where she was and what she was doing.

"What's wrong?" Tessa asked.

Mum threw the clothes in Tessa's direction and whirled around. "Coffee," she said, stomping out of the room, sounding as if she had a bad cold.

Clearly something was wrong. Tessa hurried to change into the dry clothes on her way to the kitchen.

Mum stood with her back to Tessa, making a mug of black coffee and a cup of hot chocolate. When she trudged to the table, her eyes were glassy. Tessa snuggled into the pile of cushions in the corner of the bench, feeling her own tears rising.

Mum took a big gulp of coffee. "Oma might need heart

surgery," she said. "They're transferring her to the University Heart Clinic in Innsbruck tonight."

Tessa slumped back and leaned her head against the wall. Her plan of making Oma feel better by keeping the promise to Opa was stupid. And Oma didn't even know she'd delivered the berries. She took a sip of her hot chocolate, burning her tongue, and watched blurry teardrops splatter onto her red knitted top.

"Maybe her heart is broken because Opa died."

"Maybe, sweetheart." Mum smiled through her tears. "Oma's heart is just a bit... The doctors need to fix it. They *can* fix her heart."

Tessa didn't know if Mum was trying to convince herself or Tessa. They sat in silence for a while.

"I'll be staying at Cousin Sonja's in Innsbruck for a few days, and I want to get there tonight. I talked to Lisa's mum on the way home—"

"No."

"Tessa..."

"We're not friends, Mum. I don't mind being home alone."

"Please, Tessa. Don't be difficult. You can't stay here on your own."

"Then let me come! I want to be with Oma."

Mum smiled, but shook her head.

"What about Aunt Annie and Uncle Harry?" It would give her an opportunity to spy on the skier from the avalanche... What was wrong with her, she wondered. How could she think about that, when Oma was in the hospital?

"I'm sure Annie's busy. They're bound to be fully booked over New Year's."

"I can sleep on a mattress in Felix's room. And help Aunt Annie prepare breakfast. Please, Mum." Tessa leaned across the table and took Mum's warm hands in hers. For a moment their roles seemed to have been switched. "Please. Then you don't need to worry about me at all."

Mum sniffed and wiped her tears away with a dishcloth. "I suppose I could ask. They'd want to know about my mum's surgery anyway."

It took Tessa two minutes to stuff the elf book, a toothbrush, and some clean clothes into a duffle bag. Mum's choked voice, as she explained the situation to Aunt Annie, came through her bedroom door.

At least she could let Oma know that she'd delivered the berries. She sat down at her desk and tore a piece of checkered paper from her math workbook. At the top, in red marker, she wrote, GET WELL SOON OMA, inside a heart. Below, in pencil, she drew a row of nine empty horizontal boxes, counting, while she mumbled the letters, "b-a-r-b-e-g-a-z-i." She had little time and now came the difficult part. Oma was so much better than her at crossword puzzles.

Tessa needed help, and she grabbed the Scrabble box and poured the tiles onto the table. On the board, she built her message: BARBEGAZI HAVE BERRIES PROMISE TO OPA KEPT. The words didn't cross as much as Oma's secret messages usually did, but it would have to do.

"Five minutes," Mum called.

Hurriedly, she copied the pattern of boxes on the paper and added hints: type of elf, really important verb, fruits in your freezer, something you say you will do, opposite of from, grandfather, past of keep.

Mum glanced at the piece of paper when Tessa gave it to her and said, "Oh, you've made her a crossword," before she folded it and slid it in between the pages of the novel in her handbag. "She'll be so pleased."

When Mum dropped Tessa at Felix's house before she drove to Innsbruck, Felix was already asleep—it was late and he'd done extra training in the afternoon—so Tessa would sleep on the sofa in the lounge this first night.

After tucking blankets around her, Aunt Annie pulled a chair over to the sofa, and she sat, holding Tessa, enclosing them in a heavy lavender scent.

Tessa cried a bit. Aunt Annie sobbed violently and blew her nose, using half a box of tissues. It almost made everything worse.

When she had been pretending to sleep for a while, Aunt Annie shuffled out, leaving Tessa alone with her silent tears.

FROM *HABITS & HABITATS: A HISTORIC ACCOUNT OF ALPINE ELVES* BY PROFESSOR DR. EBERHART LUDWIG FRITZ BAHNE

Similar to polar bears, barbegazi are covered in an insulating underfur, topped by long guard hairs. Each hair shaft is transparent, with a hollow core that reflects and scatters light.

Combined with the barbegazi's ability to blend into their snowy surroundings, their hair transparency has led to legends of barbegazi being invisible.

Despite their diminutive size, barbegazi possess brutal strength, and elf researchers should at all times carry iron chains.

THURSDAY, DECEMBER 29

19

Tessa

Aunt Annie believed in the "healing powers of the great outdoors," so she sent Tessa to ski training. Also, she argued, it would take Tessa's mind off things.

Although she didn't care about the ski race any more, Tessa was glad to get away from Aunt Annie's chatter and fussing. It was too much. Luckily for Felix, Aunt Annie had a house full of guests to coddle. Tessa wondered how he managed off-season.

Felix had left early to help Coach set the course, and by the time Uncle Harry had adjusted the bindings on Felix's old skis to fit her boots and weight, she was already late.

Icy air prickled her cheeks, as she dragged herself from the bus to the lift station, puffing and exhaling white clouds. Felix's skis were heavier than her own, or perhaps her arms and back and thighs were just sore from yesterday's walk. She blamed Opa's snowshoes.

Thoughts of Opa led directly to Oma. She squeezed her

crossed fingers together, hoping the puzzle had helped, and sniffled in the chairlift.

"Just ski, Tessa," she muttered, as she set off from the top.

"Aha. Lady Tessa graces us with her presence," Coach yelled, at the start. "One hour late! Why am I standing here, if you can't be bothered to get up in the morning?"

"Sorry," Tessa mumbled. Explaining would mean tears.

"New, old skis? What happened to your Atomics?"

"Chainsaw."

Coach exploded in a roar of laughter and the queue behind her chuckled.

"Good one, Tessa," Felix called.

She got into starting position.

"What d'you think you're doing?" Coach yelled. "Glide through and inspect the course first. Take those other two late-comers with you. Explain the double gate to them."

Great. Coach had grouped her with Hans and Helmut, the two most annoying and chaotic skiers in the club. Skiing with them was like running through the village in nothing but your undies. Tessa stemmed her skis, snowplowing in slow motion down between the red and blue gates. Loud giggles from the T-bar lift told her Lisa and Maria had seen her with the two little monsters in tow.

She sped up after the course ended. Behind her, Hans and Helmut jumped on bumps and shouted and laughed. When she stopped by the lift queue, they sprayed her with snow, just as Hans skied into Helmut—or Helmut into Hans—knocking down all three of them. She disentangled herself from the rowdy mass of green arms and red legs, to disapproving noises from two German women in metallic jackets and a tall white-clad man in the queue.

At least she got her own T-bar, but the rude shouts at Bambi-legged tourists, from Hans and Helmut, embarrassed her. She hadn't brought her binoculars—she didn't need them any more—so she watched her teammates. Felix raced between the gates, almost lying on his side in every turn, sometimes touching the snow with a hand. He skied much faster than everyone else, with effortless up-down movements. No wonder he'd won the regional championship last season.

When she neared the top, she looked out into Schöngraben. Ski tracks snaked their way down all reachable sides of the gully. She hoped Gawion and the other barbegazi were safely hidden in their caves.

Tessa skied to the start of the run, with the two monsters hot on her heels.

"Okay, missy, I'm sending Hans and Helmut with you, so you'd better give it your all." Coach increased the volume. "You hear that, boys? Get her. Three, two, one, go!"

Tessa pushed off.

"Knees, Tessa! Arms, Helmut!"

She bent further down with her knees. Her aching thighs burned. The thought of the monsters behind her spurred Tessa on. Finding a rhythm, she focused her eyes on the next gate, before she even finished her current turn. Air whistled round the rim of her helmet, but she kept her focus on the course. After the finish line, she continued at full speed to the lift. Hans and Helmut hadn't caught up.

At the start, Coach stood with thumbs up on both hands, beaming at her. "See! See!" he bellowed. "That's what happens when you take your head out of the clouds."

Tessa nodded. She didn't really know what had changed, she just knew that those monsters catching up or, even worse, passing her, would've been the ultimate humiliation.

Coach gave her thumbs up on five runs before it was time to clear the piste.

The new experience of getting praise at giant-slalom training made Tessa glow inside. Perhaps things weren't completely hopeless. She had found the barbegazi. And if she could learn to race, then nothing was impossible. The doctors might even fix Oma's heart.

She couldn't help Oma, but she could at least try to help Gawion. And she knew just what she'd do when she got back to Felix's house.

20

Gawion

Brownie's nose had caught the scent of thawing spring snow, and now Gawion had proof. Real proof that Papa could not dismiss, and confirming their worst fears.

Gawion had spent the rest of the night transporting the berry gift home. The incident with the metal buckle on Tessa's pack had given his arm a numbing weakness that not even a handful of berries could dispel. Despite the pain, he managed to drag the full sky-blue carrier up to the avalanche. From there the couloirs were too steep.

Surfing downhill on the snow, even carrying an unconscious Tessa to the village, was no problem. Ascending was something else entirely. It took five trips up the steep incline, to bring all the berries to a hiding place he dug close to their cave's entrance.

He had wanted to storm inside and show Maman the gift, but stopped himself. First, he needed a plan for how to tell them. And while he lugged the heavy load up the mountain, he speculated.

Normally, he would start with bad news, then sweeten it

with good news. But his bad news was much worse than when the resting cave ceiling collapsed. Perhaps if he switched the news around, making sure everyone had a full stomach before he told them what he had discovered about Maeg... But how could he pretend food helped, when he knew the truth?

Still trying to decide, he propelled his way into the cave.

"What is this about a human helping us?" Papa asked, before Gawion had even got up off the ground. "Your whistled ramblings last night made no sense, son."

"A human! Helping us? Have you gone quite mad, Gawion? First the dogs, now this." Maman, one hand on her forehead, fanned herself with her beard. "Have we taught you nothing?"

"Never, ever, ever trust humans," Liel sing-songed, from her nest in the living cave. She played with her toy barbegazi, making it dance through a forest of bird feathers. "Never, ever trust humans, Baby," she said to the bundle of fur tied around sticks. "No, Maman," her toy answered.

"Some humans can be trusted. You trusted that human child in Vienna," Gawion said.

"That was different, son. We had known Anne since it was a mere babe."

"Well, I trust this one. Tessa is the grandchild of the berry-human. And I have a surprise for you. Wait here." Gawion scurried outside.

Behind him, Maman shrieked, "Is he bringing a human here?"

He uncovered the sky-blue carrier and snaked his way

backward through the tunnel, keeping a solid grip on the handles of the sack.

Back inside, he whistled triumphantly.

"It brought the berry gift!" Bowing, with a flourishing movement of his hand, he split the carrier open with one of his sharp claws. Clear, see-through bags tumbled out, revealing the abundance of berries.

Maman looked in wonder at the growing mountain of wild strawberries, blueberries, blackberries, and raspberries. There were even some of the large cultivated strawberries that Gawion loved.

"Nourishment," she said. "We are saved." The desperate gleam in her eyes made Gawion wonder just how close to starvation they had come.

After they had stuffed themselves with berries, contentment and calmness settled in the cave.

"The human told me they believe we are extinct," Gawion said.

A strange noise, like rumbling thunder, filled the cave as Papa exploded into a bellowing laugh.

"That is the best news I have heard in a long time," he howled.

Even Maman smiled.

"No, Papa," Liel said, her voice teary, "If we are extinct, how can I find a papa for my babies when I am a grown-up?"

"Stop being silly. We are not extinct," Gawion said, feeling exasperated.

"Come here, sweet icicle." Maman held her arms out toward

Liel. "You know, a little bird tells me how your Mont Blanc uncle and the rest of them are doing, every year before the melting starts."

Liel smiled.

"I like Gawion's human, it is just as nice as yours," she said, and licked a large strawberry. "Tell me about Anne again."

Maman gave a little chuckle.

"Oh, I remember that little human. From the moment it could walk, it followed its father around the zoological gardens. During the nine pregnancy winters it brought me the finest berries. When I vowed that my babies would not be born in captivity, Anne promised to help."

Gawion hated to ruin the mood. Brooding, he weaved the end of his beard around his berry-colored fingers. Perhaps if he waited with the bad news until nightfall...

"Gawion," Papa said. "What have you not told us?"

"I talked to the dog," he began. Of course he could not keep something so important secret from Papa, who was always watching him, waiting to point out his mistakes. Out of the corner of his eye, he saw Maman shaking her head. "It had tracked Maeg to the mountain stream below Schöngraben, close to the village."

He had expected shrieks and moans at the revelation, but Maman only whimpered and said, "I knew it."

From under the sacks of berries, he extracted the lump of Maeg's fur that Brownie had helped him retrieve.

"Bits of this clung to branches of the trees along the stream."

He gave the lump to Papa. "Higher up than Maeg would be able to reach from the ground."

"The dog told you? The exact height?" Papa glared at him, almost as if he knew how Gawion had jumped and jumped to pluck the fur. "Because you did not cross the boundary last night, did you?"

Gawion swallowed. "I..." He nodded slowly, staring down at his speckled beard.

Papa took a deep breath.

"So someone carried her. Could she have placed the fur herself?"

Gawion shrugged. "Perhaps."

"Maybe Maeg also met a nice human," Liel said, but even she seemed to sense the fear reigniting in their home.

"The berry-human's grandchild will search in the village. I am meeting it in the evening, by the earth mounds."

"For the love of snow, you are too trusting." Maman shook her head again. "The human might contrive to capture you."

"It would never do that, Maman," Gawion said, with a certainty he did not quite feel.

21

Tessa

Tessa trudged after Felix, from the bus stop. They walked in silence past hotels and pensions displaying red *Fully booked* signs. She sagged farther and farther behind until Felix waited by the corner of the long, steep driveway up to Berger's Bed and Breakfast.

"Take these, I'll take your skis." He held his poles toward her. "Just don't expect me to do it again, noodle-arms."

Tessa was so tired she didn't argue.

"So what really happened to your own skis?" He heaved both pairs of skis onto his shoulders and walked on. "Dad said he'd never seen anything like it."

"Chainsaw." Tessa made an odd-sounding fake laugh. She needed time to think. She couldn't tell Felix about the barbegazi, but she didn't want to lie to him either.

"It wasn't one of your barbie-fairies?"

"I thought you didn't believe me."

"Whatever." Felix shook his head.

"Is that skier from the avalanche still at your house?"

"I guess. Mum lets the rooms for the whole week in high season."

They rounded the bend, and the house rose above them. With its thick layer of fairytale snow frosting, the oversized roof sparkled in the sun. Car-shaped white mounds stood in a row along the driveway and on the track up to Schöngraben.

"Which room is it?" Tessa asked, searching the dark windows below the garlands of snow.

"Which room is what?"

"That skier's."

"It's on the other side. The corner toward Schöngraben. Why?"

"No reason."

Inside, the house was silent. No sounds came from the guest rooms upstairs. With the sun shining in a clear blue sky, the guests—tourists who skied for fun, one week a year—would spend the whole day on the slopes.

Aunt Annie had left them a note—that she was visiting Aunt Margit, one of the numerous relatives living in the valley—and a homemade lasagna. They didn't bother heating the food, but gulped it down with large glasses of blackcurrant cordial.

After lunch, Felix wanted to do his knee bend exercises and rope jumps, and play on his computer. Tessa said she'd relax on the sofa for a bit. As soon as his bedroom door was closed, though, she sneaked upstairs, where the guest rooms were, and along the narrow corridor, her stockinged feet making soft swishing sounds against the carpet. She whistled, hoping the tune didn't mean anything offensive to a barbegazi, and listened for an answer. Nothing. After knocking, she tried a few doors, but they were locked.

Aunt Annie ruled her kingdom from the kitchen. That's where the master key would be. Tessa went downstairs, tiptoeing past Felix's door, even though she could hear the rhythmic stamps of his exercises. In the kitchen, she opened cupboard after cupboard until she found one with a neat row of empty numbered nails. At the end hung a key with no number. The master key.

Her fingers hovered in front of the key before she snatched it from the nail.

"What're you doing? Are you crazy?" said Felix, who'd entered the kitchen, wrestling the key from her.

"Please! Just let me peek into his room. I won't even go in."

"Why?"

"It's a long story." She really wanted to keep the barbegazi a secret, but if Maeg was here, she might need Felix's help. If Maeg wasn't, she needn't tell him anything. "I'll explain after."

"I'm not supposed to use the master key when there are guests," he mumbled.

"No one will know."

"Promise you won't go inside." Felix held the key toward her.

Tessa tried taking it, but Felix clutched the key until she said, "Promise."

"Be quick. I'll whistle if anyone comes." He sat down on the bottom step of the staircase. "It's the last door."

Upstairs again, her heart pumped as if she was in the middle of a ski race. She lay both palms and her ear against the door, listening. After knocking again, her shaking hand guided the key into the lock and turned it. Blood hammered at her temples as she pushed the door open.

"Hello... Maeg?" she said, and whistled a single tone.

A sliver of sunshine came through the drawn curtains. At first glance, from the doorway, the tidy room seemed empty, except for a closed suitcase on the bench. The only clutter was on the desk, where a ski helmet with silvery goggles perched. Tessa had wanted those goggles for Christmas, but Mum said they were too expensive. Dad would've bought them, but she hadn't asked him. The trendy goggles confirmed her suspicions —this guest was one of those cool off-piste skiers.

Something shiny on the chair reflected the light, but, in the gloom, she couldn't see what it was.

"Tessa?" Felix called from below.

She had to see what was on that chair. It might be important. She wouldn't touch anything, and neither Felix nor the guest would know she'd been in the room. "Just a moment."

After casting a glance back down the vacated corridor, Tessa tiptoed into the room and eased the chair out from underneath the desk. Icy prickles tingled on her back. A heavy, metal chain and a sharp iron poker lay on the seat.

Skiers had no use for metal chains and pokers, but people hunting barbegazi did. This was evidence.

Tessa rushed to open the wooden wardrobe. Ironed shirts and trousers hung above stacks of folded pullovers and socks. Otherwise it was empty. She opened the bathroom door and looked behind the shower curtain. She got down on all fours, searching under the bed and the desk. Nothing. The suitcase was locked. She shook it. From inside, came the sound of clanking metal. Where could Maeg be?

Felix called again, but she ignored him and opened the desk drawer. On top of a stack of papers was a worn terrain map. A scatter of black circles and red crosses marked spots on the clustered contour curves. It was a map of Schöngraben.

"Tessa! Get out!" Felix banged his fist against the door frame. "You promised."

"Look at this." Tessa pointed to the chain and poker.

Felix sneaked closer and stared at the metal objects. "So what?"

The stairs creaked.

"Someone's coming," Felix hissed, already by the door. "Quick."

Tessa slid the chair back into place, and stuffed the map up under her knitted top. Turning to leave, her foot got stuck behind the leg of the chair. She stumbled and fell flat on the floor.

Before she could get up, a shadow from the corridor grew on the carpet and something crashed to the floor.

In slow motion, and with a sense of dread, Tessa rose.

Aunt Annie stood in the doorway, a laundry basket spilling

folded towels by her feet. Tessa had never seen Aunt Annie's face turn purple before. And her eyes were popping out of her face.

"Tessa!" she screeched. "Get out at once! Felix! What on earth are you doing?"

Felix threw the towels into the laundry basket and pulled it out of the room.

"Kitchen. Now." Aunt Annie shoved them toward the stairs before she locked the door, leaving the laundry basket on the corridor floor.

Tessa's cheeks burned like she'd just come in from the snow. The stolen map burned even more, hidden awkwardly under her top. She pushed it down into her striped long johns and moved it round to her hip.

"Never in my life... I'm disappointed in you, Felix. You know never to go into occupied guest rooms." Aunt Annie had stopped screeching, but there was an unknown sternness to her usually jolly voice. "What were you thinking?"

"It's... we—" Felix began.

"Tessa, you've had a trying week with Oma and hitting your head and everything... Perhaps you should go and lie down, have a rest." It wasn't a question. Aunt Annie looked out of the window. "Felix, get the soft brush and sweep the snow off the cars. All of them. Afterward, tidy your cave so there's room for Tessa."

Tessa scampered out of the kitchen after Felix.

"I trust you didn't touch anything in the room," Aunt Annie called behind them.

The map felt like a blinking burglar alarm.

"I'll help you," Tessa said to Felix.

"Don't. Even. Bother." He ran downstairs and slammed the door to the ski room behind him.

FROM *HABITS & HABITATS: A HISTORIC ACCOUNT OF ALPINE ELVES* BY PROFESSOR DR. EBERHART LUDWIG FRITZ BAHNE

Over long distances, barbegazi supposedly communicate with each other by whistled signals. Whether whistling, talking, or non-verbal communication is used when they are close together is unknown.

Recent reports of mountaineers in the high Alps hearing shrill whistles in advance of avalanches, has led to rumors that the barbegazi might not be extinct.

These claims are supported by the unearthing of polar-bear-like fur, by this author, in a crevasse on the glacier hiking trail between Jungfraujoch and the Konkordia Hut in Switzerland.

22

Tessa

Tessa lay on the sofa, staring at the knots in the wooden ceiling. This time, she'd really messed up. And for what? A map owned by every hiker in the area, for sale at the tourist information desk, and a chain to lock up skis. How had she ever imagined she could help Gawion find his sister?

Her phone rang. It was Mum. For a moment, she considered not answering, but then Mum would just call Aunt Annie. After the fourth ring, she picked up.

"Hi, sweetheart, how are you?"

"How's Oma?"

"Oh, you know… The doctors are very competent," Mum said, and gave a long explanation of tests and outcomes, trying to sound upbeat.

"Did she solve my puzzle? Can I talk to her?"

"She's a bit too tired to talk or do crosswords at the moment."

"Please get her to do it, Mum. It'll make her feel better."

Mum ended the call with, "I hope you're being a big help to Annie."

Tessa hadn't thought she could feel any worse.

She went to the window. Blankets of winter snow still hid half the cars, and a cloud of powder surrounded Felix. It was unfair only he got punished. Perhaps he'd cooled off by now and would let her take over.

Outside, the sun had disappeared and the temperature dropped.

Felix greeted her with a "Go away", without even pausing in his work.

"I want to help."

"You'll just scratch the cars."

Frost bloomed like flowers of ice on the windscreens of the cars Felix had already uncovered. Tessa shuddered, remembering dark mornings, driving to school in the car when Mum had left it outside during the night.

Of course! She almost laughed out loud. You couldn't keep a barbegazi inside a house. They'd never survive the heat. But in one of these frozen cars…

As inconspicuously as possible, she ambled up along the row of visible cars, whistling a few notes. At each one, she ducked behind them and made peeking holes on the windows with her warm breath, before examining the interior. One car had a white sweater on the backseat, and she took so long to be sure it wasn't Maeg that Felix had walked up to her and poked her shoulder with the brush.

"Stop touching the cars. What're you doing?"

"Looking for the car of that guest."

"Okay, Tessa, I'll play along in your spy game. Just tell me why."

It wasn't a game. If Felix knew what was happening, he wouldn't be so condescending. He'd be helping her search for Maeg. But she couldn't tell him without betraying Gawion's trust.

"Show me the car first," she said.

"It's not here."

"You're sure?"

Felix rolled his eyes.

"First of all, it's not a car, it's a white van. The coolest van ever. With tinted windows, four-wheel drive, four-liter engine." He counted out these facts on his gloved fingers. "I haven't seen it since he arrived. Probably scared of the other guests denting it."

Tessa's mind whirled. Maeg had disappeared on Monday. A van was an even better hiding place than a car. But it could be anywhere: on a lift station parking lot, on a forest track, by a hotel or post office or supermarket in one of the nearby villages. How would she ever find it? She didn't even know what to look for.

But Felix did. She needed his help, and she owed him an explanation. Even if it meant trusting him with the secret of the barbegazi.

While he swept snow off the last cars, she told him everything that had happened in the last two days. She didn't mention Brownie. Talking with a dog might be too big of a stretch for Felix.

Afterward, Tessa sat on his bed while he tidied his room, telling him barbegazi facts she'd learned from her elf book. Felix collected a jumble of clothes and shoes and comic books from the floor, and stuffed everything into his wardrobe. Signed posters of seven World Cup skiers hung on the walls. Two monitors, keyboards, a steering wheel, and other electronic stuff crowded his desk. Using a T-shirt, he dusted his biggest skiing trophy, before he positioned it in front of his other shiny trophies, on the top bookshelf.

"I don't know, Tessa," he said, pulling on the T-shirt over his long thermal top. "If Dad hadn't told me about your broken skis..."

"But you saw the metal chain and poker, right? And the map—" Tessa drew the map from the inside of her long johns.

"You took that from the room? Are you insane?"

"Sorry. But look! He's marked all these places in Schöngraben." She pointed to the circles and crosses after unfolding the map. Seeing it in the light, she noticed that some of the circles had handwritten notes.

"That's funny," Tessa tapped a circle. "This one's where I fell in the hole." They both leaned over the map, trying to read the tiny scribbles.

"Willy Berger sighting," they said together.

"But that's Opa. That's where Gawion rescued him."

Felix stared at her, then he began nodding.

"Okay. I think I believe you. Let's find that van."

After he printed a photo of a similar van from the internet, they got dressed and jogged down to the huge lift station parking lot. It was late afternoon and only a few cars remained there. No white vans. They walked along the busy main road to St. Anton and back through the village, splitting up to check side streets and carparks. They didn't find the van.

Tessa's tired legs protested. Now that Felix believed her, she almost didn't mind the exhaustion. But how could they search the whole valley?

By the time they returned to the house, hunger pangs competed with her aching thighs. Aunt Annie was off on another family visit, delivering a homemade apple strudel, based on the mouth-watering smell in the kitchen. She hadn't left any of the dessert for them, but a meager plate of bread, cheese, and salami waited in the fridge.

Felix frowned. "Mum's really mad this time," he muttered.

"At least you get to meet a barbegazi," Tessa said, chewing on a wedge of Emmental cheese.

Roughly an hour before the moon would be above Eisenspitze, they mounted lightweight aluminum snowshoes—borrowed from Aunt Annie's stuff-guests-might-need closet—and hiked up the track along the mountain stream, toward the avalanche protection mounds and Gawion.

23

Gawion

A sickle moon hung low over the dreaded mountain, when Gawion surfed down toward the earth mounds, with his stomach in a knot of worry. The steep eastern gullies, with their hoof marks from agile mountain goats, remained untouched by humans. But at the bottom where Schöngraben widened, tracks from wooden feet created a detailed pattern of ridges. Hard ridges. During the day, the sun had warmed the top layer, before the rippled surface froze again. Gawion stubbed his toes on the ripples, and he whistled in pain.

"Slow down and keep your claws out, or lift your toes," Papa called.

Papa had insisted on coming with him. He mistrusted the human, and he planned to hide among the nearby trees, ready to help Gawion if needed.

It was an unnecessary precaution. Gawion did not fear Tessa, only what it might have discovered about his sister.

A shrill, human whistle rang out ahead. It had no meaning.

"Gawion," Tessa called.

Gawion sped up, then slowed as he saw that not one, but two, humans waited below in a circle of light.

Papa grabbed his arm, stopping Gawion abruptly.

"See that?" he whispered, pointing with a shaking finger. A metal chain dangled from the hand of the second human. "It is just like at Mont Blanc."

"Are you even sure it is metal, Papa?" he whispered, although the way it glinted in the light from Tessa's head and clinked when the human swung it around, left no doubt.

Papa sniffed with his large nose. Gawion just stared at Tessa. Had it deceived him? No, he refused to believe that. It had brought berries. It was a descendant of the berry-human. And that chain…

"Gaaawiiiooon," it called again.

"Fairly low iron content and rather slim," Papa said, in a low, bleak tone. "But one well-placed swipe would immobilize you long enough for them to carry you out of the gorge."

"Tessa would not do that. It wants to find Maeg."

"Who chose to meet so near the village, son?"

"But why bring us berries?"

"To gain our trust."

Gawion edged closer, trying to hear what the humans were saying. If only his hearing was as good as his sense of smell. Tessa faced away from him, and he could not make out its words.

The other human swung the scary chain faster and faster. Raising its voice, so they heard every word, it spoke with an angry undertone. "D'you know how many barbarians I could've killed while we're standing here? If that barbegazi isn't coming, this is a complete waste of time. Capture it on your phone. Or bring it to the house and hide it in the shed."

Gawion stopped breathing. The forest stilled, as if the trees were listening. As if like him, they were trying to understand the strange language. Trying to find an explanation that was not the obvious meaning of those words. But there was no other explanation. The new human talked about killing, and hiding him in a shed, and capturing him on a phone—whatever that was.

Tessa stomped. Its feet clanked. The wooden feet it had used to walk on the snow surface yesterday were gone. Tonight it wore metal feet. Metal feet primed to paralyze him with a single kick.

How could he have been so gullible? He had liked Tessa and believed its promise to help them. And here it was with an elf hunter by its side.

Papa sighed. Gawion refused to look up at him. From under his bushy eyebrows, he saw Papa shake his head.

"Come, son." Papa tugged at his arm. "I was much older than you, when humans captured me. Show me where you found the bits of Maeg's fur."

After casting a last glance at the two humans, he led Papa up through the forest, giving the earth mounds a wide berth. Behind them, Tessa continued to whistle and call his name.

Gawion swore that he would never, ever again trust a human.

24

Tessa

"**W**hy do boys always have to kill things in stupid computer games?" Tessa stepped on the spot, trying to keep warm. The snow shoes clanked. She whistled for the millionth time.

Somehow, the excitement of the afternoon had fizzled out on the way up into Schöngraben's gloom. The hike had begun with Felix asking questions about the barbegazi, which she answered. But she'd already told him everything, and soon Felix switched topics to the ski race and the pressure of being last year's seasonal champion. Tessa tried to understand, she really did, but secretly she wondered why he couldn't simply be happy about winning last year, and enjoy his collection of trophies. So they'd been standing without talking for a while when Felix lost patience and exploded into his computer game tirade.

"I play lots of games without killing," he said.

Tessa raised her voice: "Gaaawiooon!"

A long silvery chain attached Felix's house keys to his ski

trousers, and he played with it, swinging it in vertical circles, making the keys jingle. "He's not coming," he muttered, and looked at his watch. Again. "It's half past nine and the moon's already on the other side of the valley."

Tessa wiggled her fingers and toes to avoid them turning numb with cold. "Please. Let's wait a bit longer." She turned her headlamp up, enlarging the reach of the light. Rotating slowly, she stared into the shadows and repeated her call.

Felix swung his keys faster and faster. "Come on, Tessa. I want to start this season with a win, and tomorrow's the last training."

Where was Gawion? Had something happened to him? What if he'd also been taken?

"It's just a ski race," she told Felix.

"Just!" Felix rolled his eyes.

For a while, they stood in silence again. Tessa stomped her feet and swung her arms, opening them wide, then hugging herself. The chill seeped up through the thick soles of her boots. Felix just swung the chain.

"I can't play your fairy game anymore," he said eventually.

"It's not a game."

"Right now the barbarians in *Civilization* seem a whole lot more real than your barbegazi."

"They are real. I brought them berries."

"I never saw any berries. Besides, there's a hundred ways to dump a load of berries up here."

Tessa stomped harder. Why was Felix so annoying again?

"You saw the map," she said through gritted teeth.

"For all I know, you could've drawn circles on that map yourself."

Angry tears threatened, and her voice rose, turning shrill: "I didn't. You know I didn't. I found it in the room."

"Whatever. I'm not risking the race for your crazy fantasies." Felix began walking.

"Please! Wait! He'll come."

"Maria's right. You're absolutely loony," he said, without pausing, without turning, without looking at her.

Tessa's stomach clenched, like she'd been hit in the solar plexus. A chill that had nothing to do with the temperature spread from there. The light from Felix's headlamp disappeared behind the first of the avalanche mounds, and it was as if the stars had been turned off.

Felix had believed her, and now suddenly he didn't. He thought she was loony. Everyone did.

Why would Gawion trust her? He needed someone to help save his sister, and Tessa couldn't help anyone. She couldn't help him and she couldn't help Oma.

How could she have thought a silly crossword puzzle would make any difference?

Warm tears splashed down her cheeks as the last of her resolve melted away. She sobbed into her gloves and slumped until she sat on her knees, the snowshoes forcing her to angle her feet awkwardly. Her knees grew colder and colder, prickling until they turned numb, and then she didn't feel them at all. If only the pain inside could disappear as easily.

The blood flowing toward her chest would never be enough to fill two holes in her heart.

FROM *HABITS & HABITATS: A HISTORIC ACCOUNT OF ALPINE ELVES* BY PROFESSOR DR. EBERHART LUDWIG FRITZ BAHNE

Barbegazi have elfish abilities for languages and can speak in whichever tongue they are addressed, as documented in Foubergé's transcriptions from 1779.*

To the frustration of more recent elf researchers, barbegazi refuse to talk in captivity. In the only successful case of getting a response, the scientist used a modified replica of "the rack" found in the Tower of London, to stretch the feet of the barbegazi, until it screamed: "Zooterkins! Gadzooks! Potzblitz! Gadsbudlikins!"

After the demise of the creature, a linguist read the transcripts, believed to be gibberish, and explained that these were perfectly normal swear words from the Renaissance period.

---

*Foubergé, A.S. 1779: "An Examination of the Usage of Language by Subhuman Creatures" from *Philosophical Transactions*, Vol. 69. London: Royal Society, 721–748

25

Gawion

Gawion glided in front of Papa, on the narrow track between the mountain stream and the forest. Next to Brownie's deep paw prints, large indents, not much deeper than their own shallow marks, made a pattern in the snow—the footprints from Tessa's and the elf hunter's surface-walking metal feet.

They stopped, and, after crawling up on Papa's back, Gawion snatched a lump of fur from a branch.

Papa sniffed it, inhaling deeply while shaking his head.

"I refused to believe it," he said. "I hoped she was merely injured..." Then he ordered Gawion to go home, while he searched near the human habitats. "Await my whistle, when the brightest stars of Ursa Major are above Polaris," Papa called, on his way down the track.

Gawion was so downcast he did not even protest. He shuffled up between the trees, staying in the forest high above the earth mounds. He wondered what he was supposed to do if Papa did not whistle at the agreed time: Search for him or hide?

Through the dark, needle-covered twigs, he saw a faint light shining. At least Tessa had stopped whistling and calling his name. A weird gurgling sound—a cross between a bubbling spring and an animal in pain—reached him. It was unlike anything he had ever heard, and it seemed to be coming from the humans.

Curious, he crept nearer, promising himself to stay in the shadows.

The elf hunter had disappeared. Rolled up like a colored snowball, Tessa lay on the ground, convulsing, and emitting the strange loud gurgles. It must be very cold after so long in the snow. Suddenly it howled like a wolf. The howl meant nothing in Wolfish, but it was clearly a cry of pain. Had the elf hunter attacked Tessa? Or was it all another trick, to trap him with?

Gawion inhaled, filling his nostrils with night-forest air. His nose only detected a weak metallic taint. Much less than the smell from that chain. The human had saved them from starvation—he could not just leave it to die in the cold.

He circled Tessa widely, sniffing, ready to scamper at any sign of danger. Not daring to approach, in case it kicked him with those clanking feet, he called its name.

Three times he called, before it reacted. The light from Tessa's head traveled over the snow until he felt the slight tingle of its feeble warmth.

"Oh. Gawion. Where. Were. You?" Tessa said, between bouts of the weird gurgles.

"Where is the elf hunter?"

"In the village. We haven't found Maeg yet."

"Why did you bring it here?" Gawion spoke with Papa's sternness.

"The elf hunter? Here? No. You misunderstand. That's Felix. He's helping us. He was, anyway..." Mountain springs streamed down Tessa's cheeks.

Perhaps trusting a human was naive, but he could tell this sadness was real. Gawion lumbered closer.

"You thought I'd brought the elf hunter? To capture you? You don't trust me?" Tessa's speech ended with another howl, as piercing as that of a fox he had once heard, after one of her cubs had been killed by a human vehicle.

"No, no. I do trust you," he said, "Only my father was with me and... and we thought the... the metal chain." It seemed silly, now, to have been scared of this baby human.

"...And my Oma's in the hospital and her heart's broken, and I don't know what to do." It gurgled again.

He stroked one of its braided side-beards. Slowly the streams became trickling springs and the only sounds were wet sniffs from its pointy nose.

Tessa got up, wiping its eyes.

"The elf hunter is staying in Felix's house," it told him. "That's why I needed his help. Will you come with me?"

Gawion hesitated. They had talked about bringing him to a shed. Was this all part of a plan?

"If we run, we might catch Felix before he gets home."

"I have a better idea." The faster they caught this Felix, the farther they would be from the village. "If you leave the metal feet here, I can carry you."

With one pull at a strap by each ankle, Tessa let the metal feet drop to the ground.

"Cool! I don't remember last time you carried me."

When he scooped Tessa up, it gave a small shriek. Its warmth burned in his arms. Gawion leapt forward to gain initial speed, then surfed over the rippled surface, remembering to lift his toes. The bundle he carried made new bubbling noises, with no sadness to them.

Outside the earth mounds, Tessa directed him east of the mountain stream where he had just been. He hoped Papa was far away by now.

Near an illuminated human habitat, a light bounced ahead of them, and Tessa called, "Feeeliiix!"

"What?" The beam swirled toward them. The other human stood transfixed until Gawion stopped next to it with a sideways skid.

It gaped so much he could see the human's single row of teeth, its raspberry-colored tongue, and, worst of all, the inside of its throat. It really ought to hide that view behind a beard. Gawion averted his eyes.

Tessa slid down from his arms, saying, "You still think I'm loony?"

"What... It's... I... You're real," it sputtered, and finally closed its mouth.

Perhaps it was a less intelligent human than Tessa. It was certainly not scary.

"Sorry, Tessa," it said.

"Gawion, meet Felix," Tessa continued. "Felix, put your key chain away, it's made with iron, and barbegazi don't like iron."

Still staring at him, Felix folded the frightening metal chain and hid it in a flap in its clothes.

"Felix lives right there." Tessa pointed at the glare behind the trees. "I found a map and some iron tools in the elf hunter's room, and I'm sure he's got Maeg in his van."

Van? Gawion ran through a list of meanings for the word. A bird's wing. A vanguard. None of them made sense.

"May I ask what a van is?"

"It's a big car. A vehicle. Look," Felix said, and pulled a strange flat image out of a pocket. "This one's white, with tinted windows so you can't see what's inside."

"I see," he said, rather relieved that the cousin could speak in full sentences and keep its mouth reasonably closed. "And where is this van?"

"We don't know," Tessa explained. "We've been searching all afternoon."

"My father and I can continue the search. But extracting Maeg from a metal vehicle might require your assistance."

"If you find the van, we'll think of a way of getting your sister out," Tessa said.

"Just come and get us. Throw something at my window to wake us up," Felix said. "I'll show you."

Both humans turned off their lights and ran to the last tree before the house, a huge pine. They crept under its prickly branches. Gawion followed them.

Felix pointed. "The window on the corner is my room." It rummaged in the darkness and found one of the hard ovals Liel loved to play with. "Can you hit it with a pine cone?"

It was not a snowball, but Gawion and Maeg had often thrown them at each other, whenever the snow was too wonderfully cold to make snowballs. He took the oval, crept out of the den under the tree, brought the thing back over his shoulder and sent it off with a spin.

It hit the dark square with a clank.

Felix whistled two shrill tones. It sounded almost as if it whistled "hot glacier," which made very little sense. He was about to ask Felix what it meant, when a human appeared by the entrance to the habitat. Artificial light spilt out on its snowy hair and new-snow colored garments. Gawion ducked back under the sheltering twigs. The human rounded the corner, and stared at the dark square Gawion's oval had hit. Then it turned toward the mountains, toward the trees, toward them.

"It's him," Felix whispered.

Tessa leaned forward.

"I think I've seen him before."

Gawion had seen that particular human before. Several times, in fact, over the past decades. He had walloped it once. Now he wished he had never dug it out of the avalanche. He knew it by the tilt of its shoulders and the length of its legs, but most of all he knew it by its scent. A scent that now had a distinct flavor of Maeg.

"The elf hunter," he hissed.

"I thought he was much younger," Tessa whispered.

The elf hunter turned back, climbed up to the entrance, and disappeared into the dwelling.

"No," Felix said, "that's him. That's Professor Bahne."

FRIDAY, DECEMBER 30

26

Gawion

Gawion stood on an outcrop in the forest above the village, gazing up at the Great Bear in the sky. It hung upside down directly above Polaris.

Papa ought to whistle soon. Gawion could not wait to speak with him. Papa would be astonished, when he learned how Gawion's human friends had tracked down the elf hunter, and worked out where it kept Maeg captured.

Waves of heat prickled under his soles, when he remembered how the elf hunter had just appeared out of nowhere, while he stood next to that big tree, exposed. He had wanted to rush after it, into the human habitat, and force the monster to reveal where it held his sister.

Tessa had seemed to be as shocked as he was, while Felix had taken charge and held Gawion back.

"Professor Bahne?" Tessa had repeated. "But..."

"Professor Bahne is the elf hunter, and he's here. That means

Maeg's here. Somewhere. We'll find her," Felix had said, patting his shoulder, calming him.

Tessa's eyebrows had scrunched together, rippling its forehead.

"Take the printout. And wake us when you find the van." Felix had rolled the strange flat image of the vehicle into a hollow cylinder, and Gawion had dropped it in his beard pocket.

Tessa had nodded slowly, but still said nothing, while he agreed with Felix to return the following evening, if they did not find the van during the night.

When Gawion had set off, bouncing from foot to foot up through the forest, there had been a new lightness to his step. Felix had made it sound as if it was only a matter of time before they found Maeg. Perhaps it was. They only needed to locate the vehicle. Papa would be so relieved! He might even admit that he had been wrong to doubt Gawion's judgement.

Finally, Papa whistled. He was in the same forest as Gawion, farther down in the valley, and it did not take long to find him. But the moment Gawion said he had talked to the two humans, Papa exploded in a stream of hissed reprimands. Rebukes for not going straight home and for talking to humans and dogs segued into a general scolding for trusting humans.

"I suppose it is our own fault for living in a place with no other children," he hissed.

"I am not a child," Gawion said, before he told Papa about the elf hunter, and showed him the image of the new-snow-colored vehicle.

Papa frowned and shook his head, muttering: "A human has abducted your sister, and you want me to trust human children?"

At least he did not send Gawion home.

Staying by the edge of the forest, they glided past villages and empty fields, far down into the inhabited valley. They stopped and sneaked closer to investigate, whenever they saw clusters of human vehicles. But their search yielded no result. The only vehicle they discovered that resembled the flat image was as dark as a starless night.

When dawn broke, and they returned to the cave, Gawion's hope of finding Maeg had shrunk to something smaller than a blackberry at the bottom of a gorge.

Throughout the morning, Maman kept nagging him. And Liel, with her constant background chant of "never, ever trust a human," really got on his nerves.

"You know nothing of humans," he finally shouted, and kicked the big ice cooler, knocking a third off it. "Potzblitz! I cannot wait to get my own cave. I am sick of—"

Papa whistled so piercingly then that lumps of snow fell from the ceiling, and the tunnel entrance to the cave collapsed.

"You can build one right now," he bellowed. "And take your sesquicentennial hormones with you."

Seething with anger, Gawion marched into the resting cave.

"And this!" Papa sent the piece of broken-off ice cooler spinning across the floor after him. Gawion jumped out of the way, and it continued into the soft snow, making a barbegazi-foot-deep hole.

"Thanks for the help," he muttered.

Behind him, Maman said, "Oh, Aeglosben, the humans might have heard that whistle."

For the rest of the day, Gawion worked hard. He started by digging a long, long tunnel from the resting cave. Next came his very own exit. He needed to get rid of the excess snow, and he shoveled it up to the surface with his feet. Papa surely had not considered that he would now be able to leave unnoticed, he thought, when he broke through the surface into a downpour of wonderful white pellets.

Every time Gawion scooped powder snow out, he hoped to see the sky had darkened, so he could return to Tessa and Felix.

27

Tessa

Aunt Annie's anger evaporated while they helped her slice cucumbers, and carry jugs of milk and juice, for the breakfast buffet. She believed their hasty explanation of wanting to get to training early, and they left when the first guest appeared in the breakfast room.

Outside, only a single pine cone lay below Felix's window—Gawion had not returned. Hidden behind the same large pine tree that had concealed them last night, they folded printed photos of a van similar to Bahne's.

"I still can't believe Professor Bahne might be the elf hunter," Tessa said.

"Might be?" Felix crammed the printouts into his pocket. "The evidence is clear."

"Hmmm. And I can't believe you never told me he was the skier in that avalanche."

"And I can't believe you never told me who'd written that book." Felix mimicked her voice in a mocking tone.

Tessa's helmet dangled from her arm, but she wore her normal boots. Her ski boots lay by her side, unbuckled, ready to put on if Bahne appeared in his skiing gear.

"Sure you don't want me to come?" Felix asked, for the millionth time.

Tessa nodded.

"Just tell Coach I have a stomach bug, and hand out those photos. Promise the finder a full baking tray of Aunt Annie's brownies." That ought to get their teammates interested in searching for the van. "Anyway, you need the training more than me." She winked.

Felix punched her shoulder.

"Text me," he said, before picking up his skis and setting off.

She waited impatiently, stamping her feet and blowing fake smoke signals in the frozen air. Guests stumbled out of the house, balancing skis and poles and children, and slid toward the ski bus. No matter how many times she turned it over in her head, Tessa couldn't grasp that she'd been deceived. When no one except Oma believed her, Bahne's book had given her hope. She'd planned to write to him, *trust* him with her knowledge of the barbegazi. And she refused to believe she'd been hoodwinked. There had to be another explanation.

When Bahne finally left the house in his white outfit, he wore normal boots, and he didn't bring skis. He stared at the mountains surrounding Schöngraben before he turned and strode down the driveway. Tessa dumped the helmet next to her boots and skis, and followed him.

After crossing the road, he paused by the bus stop. Tessa hid behind the bustle of people waiting for the bus to the lifts. Before he walked on, he glanced back over his shoulder. She ducked, although he wouldn't recognize her if he saw her in the crowd.

No one looked less like a crazy off-piste skier than the professor. In fact, he resembled an elderly gentleman, a village doctor, in one of Oma's TV series. He certainly didn't look like a barbegazi abductor. And maybe he wasn't one. Maybe they'd come to all the wrong conclusions. What evidence did they really have? A scent in the air, detected only by Gawion. An iron chain and an old map—part of the research for his latest book, perhaps.

Without looking back, Bahne turned down Tessa's own street. Shadowing him, she tried to act like a tourist. A boring gray jacket and round retro sunglasses from Aunt Annie's stuff-guests-might-need closet served as her disguise.

Bahne strode right past her house, with its unlit fairy lights around the black windows, and turned left down a bend in the road. Her stomach knotted. Would Oma be having heart surgery today? She crossed her fingers on both hands, whispering, "Please, let Oma be okay."

By the garage, she stopped and peeked round the corner. The street turned a sharp left, downhill, and ended in the small parking lot by the Matthis Bed and Breakfast. Expecting Bahne to come driving up the hill, Tessa stayed hidden next to the garage. She checked the time on her phone and inspected the photo Felix had sent of the van.

If only she could find another explanation. What if someone

else had also been in the avalanche? What if Professor Bahne was hunting the elf hunter? Perhaps he was another secret barbegazi protector. So secret, even the barbegazi didn't know of his existence.

After five minutes, Tessa traipsed back to the corner. With nowhere to hide, she practiced things to say if Bahne confronted her on the road. Things like "I'm staying at Matthis's. I forgot my lift card." It was stupid. He didn't know her, and he had no reason to confront her.

Six cars, blanketed in snow, stood in the parking lot. No vans. Bahne had disappeared.

Was he in the house? Had he booked two rooms? Not likely. Mrs. Matthis would've told the whole village, if an even remotely interesting guest stayed with them. Where had he gone? If she'd lost him, Felix would be really impressed...

Then she saw a white figure, hurrying along the trodden trail that crossed the snow-covered fields. She hid behind a low wall, got her binoculars out and had an instant close-up view of the frozen valley. No ray of sun reached the bottom of it between early December and the end of January, and the air remained still and icy during those months. It was the perfect place to stash something in sub-zero temperatures.

Bahne crossed the main road and vanished down the hiking trail. Tessa clambered over the wall, and sprinted after him over the fields and across the road. Half-skidding, she followed the steep trail under the railway overpass, to the wooden bridge crossing the river.

The track up to the sawmill was partly hidden by towering stacks of planks covered in fluttering tarpaulins. On the far side of the bridge, the cross-country ski trail ran alongside the rushing water and a steep hiking route led up into the forest. Above her, a train whooshed by.

There was no sign of the professor.

Paw prints and footprints and markings from ski poles surrounded the trail. Pine needles lay scattered on some, and others had a half-erased, day-old look to them. She chose a set of fresh footprints to follow, and jogged toward the sawmill.

When she passed the dark office building, she paused to glance at a closed-for-the-holidays sign, with a sprig of holly attached to it, on the main door, before she continued through the maze of sheds and silent workshops. Between stacks of timber, Tessa caught a glimpse of movement. She sneaked along the heaps of wood, until she saw it. A van, exactly like the one in the photo, was parked behind an old shed, and, hidden by long rafters covered in snow, she crept closer. Close enough to hear a muffled, deep voice and metallic clanks.

What was Bahne doing in there? She wanted to text Felix, but her phone had no reception in the sheltered valley.

Try as she might, Tessa failed to find an innocent explanation for Bahne's van being parked in this remote location. Had it been any other vehicle, she could've imagined the professor confronting the elf hunter inside. But it wasn't. It was Bahne inside Bahne's van in a very cold, isolated place, and Tessa finally stopped doubting he was guilty.

One of the upright doors at the back of the van opened. Bahne crawled out backward, saying, "—get you to talk," before he slammed the door. Orange lights blinked when he locked the van with a beep. Striding past Tessa on the other side of the rafters, he mumbled to himself about some kind of rack.

She waited several minutes after he'd gone before she dashed round the shed to the van. Hiding behind it, in case Bahne returned, she tried the doors. Locked, of course. She knocked on a window. "Maeg," she said, as loud as she dared. "I'm a friend of Gawion's."

From inside came a moan and a quiet, squeaked, "Help."

FROM *HABITS & HABITATS: A
HISTORIC ACCOUNT OF ALPINE
ELVES* BY PROFESSOR
DR. EBERHART LUDWIG
FRITZ BAHNE

No accounts exist of barbegazi surviving longer than three days in temperatures above ten degrees Celsius, and they only thrive in sub-zero temperatures. Because of this heat sensitivity and their severe intolerance for iron, the recommended environment in which to keep barbegazi in captivity is an iron cage inside a glacier cave—or, these days, a ventilated, industrial freezer.

28

Tessa

Back near the road, Tessa's phone beeped as soon as she had reception. A list of messages and two missed calls from Felix appeared on the cracked screen.

What's happening? at 10:21.

Where r u? at 10:47.

U ok? at 11:03, 11:18, and 11:36.

It was almost noon now. **Ok. Found Maeg**, Tessa texted.

Meet at bus stop, he wrote back.

Tessa waited for a few minutes before Felix jumped out of the ski bus. Walking up the steep driveway to the house, Tessa had just begun telling him about her morning, when he shushed her. Bahne was walking toward them, skis on his shoulder, eyes hidden behind silvery goggles.

Tessa froze, but Felix pushed her.

"Act normal," he hissed. Then he spoke louder: "Snow's good today, Professor. Off-piste, as usual?"

"Probably." Bahne slowed, but didn't stop. "Schöngraben allows me to do what I enjoy most."

Tessa clenched her teeth. Like hunting barbegazi, she almost said.

"Just stay away from those avalanches," Felix said.

Bahne snorted. His thin mustache curled.

"How can you chat with him," Tessa said when he was out of earshot, "as if he's normal?"

Felix shrugged.

"Just thinking ahead. Perhaps we need to... I don't know... get him to talk or something."

"There you are," Aunt Annie called through a kitchen window. "Food's ready." Luckily, she turned her back before she noticed Tessa wasn't wearing the green ski-club jacket and didn't have any of her ski equipment.

After discarding their outdoor gear, Tessa and Felix entered the kitchen in their thermal long johns and knitted tops, as if they'd both just come home from training. They wolfed down spaghetti and meatballs. Tessa finished her account of the morning in whispered bursts whenever Aunt Annie, who was baking, fetched something in the pantry or turned on the mixer.

"Was the car key in his room?" Felix whispered.

Tessa thought back, trying to remember if there'd been any keys in the drawer where she found the map. She shook her head. "He could've been using it."

"We won't get the master key with Mum here anyway. I've

got another idea." Felix raised his voice to be heard over the din of the mixer. "We're going out, Mum."

"Where—" The closing door muffled the rest of Aunt Annie's question.

"Get dressed," Felix said in the hallway, "I'll get a coat hanger."

"A what?" Tessa asked, but Felix was already gone.

Outside, Felix placed a wire coat hanger against his chest before he zipped up his jacket.

"What's it for?"

"Opening the van. I saw it in an online video. Tried it once on Dad's car."

"It worked?"

"Yeah, kind of, but the alarm went off." Felix shrugged. "With Maeg inside, I'm guessing the professor has disabled his alarm."

They jogged all the way to Bahne's van. Soon Maeg would be free! Tessa couldn't wait to bring her to Gawion. He'd be so happy. And Tessa would truly become a secret barbegazi protector.

They tried the van's doors, knocked on the windows and called Maeg's name.

This time there was no answer.

"You're sure she's in there?" Felix asked.

"Still in there, you mean."

"Yeah, yeah. Anyway, with Bahne skiing, this is probably pretty safe." Felix unbent and straightened the hanger, before he attacked the passenger door.

"Perhaps she's sleeping," Tessa muttered.

After a few tries the lock sprang up. No alarm sounded. Tessa opened the door, and crawled inside and between the seats to the back.

A large cage, with rusted iron bars as thick as her wrists, filled half the space. On the floor, in the farthest corner, lay a lifeless furry bundle.

"Maeg!" Tessa tore at the locked hatch. She stretched her hand in through the bars, but the opening was too narrow for her elbow, and she couldn't reach the barbegazi. "Maeg!" she called again, a bit louder.

The bundle didn't stir.

"Let me try." Felix had joined her, and he nudged Maeg with the ex-coat-hanger before Tessa could stop him. A jolt, like an electric current, ran through the barbegazi's small body, then it stilled again. Maeg moaned.

"At least she's alive," Felix said. The lock on the cage had an old-fashioned keyhole, which he failed to open with the coat hanger. Two modern padlocks on massive iron chains further secured the hatch. "Pro stuff! No chance opening these with any of Dad's tools. We need the keys."

"I promise, we'll save you, Maeg," Tessa whispered, as she crept out of the van.

They trudged between locked sawmill buildings and stacks of planks, the gushing river swallowing the sound of their footsteps. Scenarios for rescue missions flitted through Tessa's mind, but none of them were realistic. She discarded them faster than they took to appear.

Halfway home, they sought cover from an icy drizzle under the wide eaves of a house. Here, Aunt Annie couldn't overhear them, and so they leaned against the wall to think up a plan. A few times one of them began a sentence with "What if?..." only to end it with "...Forget it."

Eventually the streetlights flickered on. Sleet pounded on the roof. Tessa was numb with cold when an idea finally took form.

"This might sound really crazy..." she said, "and we would need Gawion's help. And lots of luck."

Without delay, she told Felix her plan.

29

Professor Bahne

After closing the door, Bahne turned the key twice and tested the handle. He surveyed the room. His locked suitcase, with his tools and fur samples, lay at the exact angle he had placed it before going out. Everything seemed to be in order, unlike yesterday.

Yesterday, an unfamiliar scent had lingered in the room, and his suitcase had been moved. When he confronted Mrs. Berger this morning, she denied that anyone had been inside, but there was something shifty to her eyes. Perhaps, he thought, he should leave this place earlier than planned.

At home, in his laboratory, he had an industrial walk-in freezer and the necessary equipment to force the barbegazi to talk. A local builder had replicated the modified rack, based on a sketch from the historic archives in Geneva. His own narrow feet tingled, at the mere thought of stretching those hairy barbegazi pads.

"But how can I keep it alive?" he muttered. Even after years of trawling through ancient texts, their dietary needs remained an unsolved mystery. He emptied the contents of his backpack. Moss, bark, pine cones, pine needles, and grass from deep below the snow in Schöngraben scattered onto the plastic sheet on top of his bed. Despite trying to feed it a variety of native plants, the barbegazi in his van was weak from lack of sustenance. So far, it had rejected everything he offered, except a few ice cubes. Whatever the barbegazi needed, he knew it must be available here and now in these mountains. And so, instead of leaving early, he might have to extend his stay.

While he showered and changed clothes, he took deep breaths, and reminded himself that despite his failure to get any human words out of the barbegazi, his trip was an immense success.

All the miserable Christmas holidays he had spent in this B & B, with its chatterbox proprietor, had finally paid off. After years of marking barbegazi tracks on his map, he had known the most likely places to be rescued by one of them.

"Rescued," he scoffed. As if he needed to be rescued. His new avalanche airbag had worked like a charm. It had kept him afloat on the surface of the sliding snow. Both skis were gone, as expected, but he would rather lose them than risk breaking a leg. And he had, of course, brought snowshoes. Pretending to be unconscious until he could get his iron chain around the barbegazi had been easy.

Preventing it from starving to death was turning out to be difficult.

But even if the services of a taxidermist would be required, the discovery and capture of a barbegazi was a breakthrough for science. A crowning end to his career. The means to restoring his professional reputation and making his colleagues across Europe envious. He sneered, imagining the astounded faces of the old guard, all those who usually snickered behind his back at zoological conferences, convinced elves were as extinct as the dinosaurs.

He alone had been certain the barbegazi were still alive. When the institute stopped funding his barbegazi research a decade ago, he continued the hunt. And every year he spent time in locations with barbegazi rumors: skiing in St. Anton over Christmas and in Chamonix during Easter, and crossing the Swiss Alps on glacier hiking trails every weekend in summer and autumn.

After sitting down at the desk, he opened the drawer and extracted his black fountain pen. Unfortunately, he had no need for the red pen today. He only wanted to mark a few new crevices without barbegazi traces on the map. The map. Bahne flipped through the stashed papers twice, without finding it.

He struck the desk with a white-knuckled fist, saying aloud, "They are all liars."

Someone had been in his room and taken his map. Mrs. Berger had been lying. Just like old Willy Berger had lied when he denied being rescued by a barbegazi. Even mentioning it in *Habits & Habitats* had not brought the stubborn mountain man to his senses.

Bahne stood up abruptly. The chair snagged on the carpet

and crashed to the floor. He picked up his notebook and strode out of the room, letting the door slam.

Maybe from the armchair in the breakfast room, he might overhear something that could lead him to the map thief.

30

Tessa

Icy pellets of hail attacked them on their way home. A bang rang out, nearby. Blurry green sparkles lit up the dark sky—an impatient child setting off early New Year's fireworks.

"Let's hope Bahne isn't here yet," Tessa said. She planned to wait for him in the ski room. "And for lots of snow and avalanches."

Felix punched in the code by the back door. "You *are* loony," he said, with a hint of admiration.

Yells warned them of the mayhem inside. A frantic mum unbuckled the tiny ski boots on her wailing toddler and wiped goo from its nose at the same time. Two drenched boys in ski boots fought, using poles as swords.

Luckily, it only took them a second to find Bahne's white ski boots on the boot heater. Unluckily, that meant he was already home, and Tessa needed to revise her plan.

Upstairs, Bahne was sipping a cup of tea in front of the fire in the breakfast room, a notebook in his lap. Unable to believe her luck, Tessa made straight for him, but was intercepted by Aunt Annie, who pulled her into the kitchen and shut the door.

"What on earth do you think you're doing?"

"I just want to ask Bahne—"

"Professor Bahne. Don't bother him. Can't you see he's working?" She sighed. "Wouldn't it be wonderful if he wrote his next book here by my fire?"

"But—"

Aunt Annie cut her off. "No buts. He's a valued guest. Not like them. Bless the poor mother." She nodded toward the noisy ski room. "Professor Bahne is a distinguished gentleman who doesn't want to be disturbed. Especially not by children." She shooed Tessa back into the hallway.

Over her shoulder, Tessa saw Bahne vacate the chair by the fire and walk up the stairs to the guest rooms. No wonder, with the racket from the ski room.

Later, she sat on the floor of Felix's bedroom, pulling her knitted thermal top over her knees. She'd just talked to Mum, who had tried to convince Tessa that her sniffling was only due to a cold.

"They might operate tomorrow." Mum sniffed and fake-sneezed. "Or Monday. I'm so glad you're at Annie's, so I don't need to fret about you."

Only about Oma. Tessa heard the unspoken words. She'd forgotten to ask if Oma had solved her puzzle, before Mum ended the call.

Felix stood by his desk, straightening the row of trophies. "What now?" he asked.

Tessa wiped her eyes. She'd have to concentrate on saving Maeg, and let Mum worry about Oma. She wound and unwound the hem of her top round her index finger.

After a while, she said, "I'll just knock on his door."

"Really? Sure you don't want me to come?"

"No. It's better if I go alone." Before she could change her mind, Tessa rose, and grabbed Opa's book and a pen from Felix's desk. "Just keep Aunt Annie down in the kitchen."

As she crept up the stairs, she heard Felix in the kitchen, saying, "Mum, can you wash my lucky ski socks? I need them for the race."

It wouldn't surprise her if he really did have lucky socks, and it didn't surprise her at all that he couldn't just wash them himself.

Walking along the corridor, music and the sound of splashing water emerged from behind one room door. From another, wails of the toddler from earlier, mixed with the older boys' laughter.

No sounds reached her from Bahne's room. Tessa stood outside it, taking deep breaths, and staring at the black book in her hand. Here goes, she thought, and knocked.

Folded paper stuck out in the middle of the book. The map. Tessa fumbled, trying to open the book while holding the pen. She'd used the map as a bookmark. Bahne's map.

On the other side of the door, heavy footsteps approached. Tessa's trembling hands dropped both pen and book. The map

fell out. As the door opened, she bent low to collect everything, and stuffed the map up under her knitted top. She hoped she hadn't stretched her top too much with her knees earlier, or the map might slip out at the slightest movement.

"Yes?"

Tessa got up from the floor, her cheeks burning. Her heart beat fast and loud like helicopter rotor blades.

"Excuse me, Professor."

He narrowed his eyes, with no movement of the thin mustache.

"Ca… can I ask you to sign this?" She shielded her face, hiding behind the book.

Bahne's expression transformed. He raised both eyebrows. It relaxed his stern features. "*Habits & Habitats.* My first book!"

Tessa struggled to remember what she'd planned to say. That blasted map. She handed him the book.

"Please?"

In his hand, it naturally fell open by the most read page. Frowning, Bahne pulled at a pair of reading glasses which hung on a cord around his neck. But as he pulled the glasses up to his eyes, a chain, hidden inside his pristine shirt, got caught up and fell out of his collar. He slipped this chain back inside his shirt a moment later, but not before Tessa had seen its set of very interesting attachments—on the end dangled three keys.

Tessa gaped, then hurried to look down at the book, while she mentally ticked off this vital item in her plan.

"What is all this?" he said, surveying the sketches and scribbles in the margins.

"My grandfather's notes. I inherited the book from him, you see. He's mentioned right there." Tessa pointed at the paragraph about Opa.

When she looked up again, Bahne was studying her.

"I'm afraid he didn't tell you the truth," she said, her heart rate speeding up again, "Because there *are* barbegazi in Schöngraben."

"He told you?"

"Yes. And I've seen them."

A gleam appeared in Bahne's eyes. "And you know where they live?"

"Well, no." She smiled inwardly at Bahne's look of disappointment. "But they come to play when I whistle." Was it too far-fetched for him to believe? She'd discussed it with Felix. But there might not be enough new snow tomorrow for avalanches.

"Play?" Bahne's eyes narrowed again.

"One of them is very funny and talks like they do in films about the Napoleonic Wars."

"It talks to you?"

"Oh yes. He's told me how his family sleep through the summer." She grasped for something from the book, something Bahne knew already, so he would believe her. Perhaps... "And how they escaped from that zoo in Vienna."

"Could you take me to meet them?" Bahne asked. "I would be very grateful. I will even mention you in my next book."

Her wish come true. How ironic.

"What's your name?" he asked her eagerly.

"Tessa. Tessa Gilbert." She bit her lip and pretended to think hard. "It's actually a secret. I promised not to tell anyone about the barbegazi," she whispered.

"You're not betraying any secrets. I already know everything about them."

Like how to make them suffer, she wanted to say, while fighting to keep her face blank. The boiling anger inside her made it difficult to speak. "Oh. Okay."

"Tomorrow morning?" he asked casually, while he opened the book at the cover and signed his name under the printed title.

"No. I have a ski race. And they don't come out until the lifts close. Do you know Kapall, Professor?" she asked, knowing that he did. It was the first place she'd ever seen him.

He nodded.

"Meet me outside the mountain hut on Kapall at half past four."

"Very well."

Tessa snatched her book away, mumbled, "Bye," and made for the stairs. As she walked, the map slipped out from under her top and fluttered to the floor. Picking it up, she glanced behind her, but Bahne was gone. She sighed with relief. Step one of the plan had worked. Now she just needed everything else to fall into place.

Only about a million things could go wrong.

31

Gawion

When the mountain transporters stopped, Papa came to inspect Gawion's work. He commented on the unevenness of the cave floor. "And the entrance tunnel is too short," he said, "Your ice block will melt."

"It is my cave." Gawion stamped on a pile of snow that had fallen from the wall, making a new, obvious bump on the floor.

Papa left without giving any further advice.

Maman brought him a handful of berries and marveled at the cave's coziness. To his surprise, she also admitted that Tessa had saved them from starvation, though she was still wary of the human.

"We are only afraid you will get disappointed," she said, caressing his beard. "Humans are so fickle, and as adults they forget the promises they made to themselves and others when they were children. At Schönbrunn, Francis Joseph visited our cage every day with an entourage of nursemaids, promising to free us upon becoming emperor, but it forgot too."

"Tessa's grandfather did not forget. Neither will Tessa."

"I dearly hope you are right." She parted her beard and removed something from it. "Give this to your human. It is a token of our indebtedness, and a promise to fulfill a wish."

Gawion stared at the precious gift in Maman's outstretched hand. "But that is fairy ma—"

"Hush. It is a snowflake charm as old as the glaciers."

"Did you make it from strands of your own beard, Maman?" he asked, unable to believe the sacrifice she had made for a human.

"The longest and strongest. True stamina."

"But your life will be shorter," he said, remembering the tales Maman had told them of the Fates spinning, measuring, and cutting threads, determining lifespans. According to the myths, these goddesses of destiny gave the barbegazi their long full beards made of stamina, and therefore their long lives.

"Only by a few years..."

"Thank you, Maman."

She tucked the gift into the pocket in his beard and fastened it with two knots.

"I still have misgivings about your human," she said. "And I beg you to stay vigilant."

———

Papa returned when darkness had fallen and insisted on accompanying Gawion to the meeting with Tessa and Felix.

Why did Papa have to treat him like a child? Why could he

not trust Gawion's judgement? Without him and his human friends, they would all be starving, and Maeg would be forever lost. Even if Maman remained skeptical of Tessa, she at least had faith in him. Papa trusted neither the humans nor Gawion.

As they made their way toward the village, a few strange lights lit up the gloom, followed by loud noise. Fireworks, ignited by humans. On one night each year, nine or ten nights after the winter solstice, the sky above the valley always erupted in a sea of colored sparkles.

Was it that time already? He remembered the solstice, and his disappointment when there was no berry gift in the hole, as clearly as if it were yesterday. But so much had happened since he met Tessa three nights ago, that it felt like they had known each other for ever. Time was like snow, sometimes fluffy and spaced out, and sometimes compressed into glaciers.

Papa hid between the trees, near the human habitat.

"I am only a whistle away." His hand clutched Gawion's shoulder. "Are you sure it is safe, son?"

"Trust me, for once," Gawion snapped.

Under the pine tree, he found one of the ovals and threw it at Felix's bright see-through wall. It bounced back with a clink. Two faces appeared, their noses pressed against the glass.

A short while later, Tessa joined him under the tree. "Felix had to help his mum," it said, then inhaled deeply, as if preparing for a long-distance whistle. "We found Maeg. She's alive, but not well. And she's in an iron cage."

Gawion choked. The blunt words smothered him with the force of a wet snow avalanche.

Tessa squeezed his hand, saying, "Don't worry. I have a plan," and told him how and where it had found Maeg, while he gasped. Then it explained the elaborate scheme to rescue his sister.

When Tessa finished talking, Gawion stared at it, amazed that a human baby could conceive of something so ingenious. Liel would not understand half of it, and she was almost fifty. He closed his mouth, pleased that his beard had hidden his gaping.

"Very cunning," he said, "I shall do my part."

Tessa blew a long puff of warm air at him. "Thank you."

There was a loud control whistle from Papa, checking in, and Gawion whistled a short, "All good" signal back.

"My only concern is the shell on the elf hunter's head," he said. "How can I remove it?"

"Shell? Oh, you mean the helmet. Wait here, I'll show you." Tessa turned and sprinted back to the habitat.

It was far from his only concern, but it was the only one Tessa could help him solve. The plan was bold. Dangerous, even. And far from infallible.

Regardless of Tessa's suggestion, he would tell Maman and Papa nothing. With their lack of faith in humans—and in him—they would doubtless forbid his participation in such a risky scheme.

32

Tessa

Tessa ran, hunchbacked, through the torrential sleet, trying to protect her ski helmet. Gawion was willing to do his part; another chunk of her plan was in place. But could he? He'd been so shocked when she told him Maeg was in an iron cage. Tessa had wanted to hug him—he'd reminded her of her favorite teddy bear. And a cuddly bear couldn't do what was required.

At least he wouldn't be alone. She'd asked him to get his parents to help. Did three cuddly barbegazi trump one evil professor?

She brushed wet branches aside and re-entered the tent-like space under the tree. Sitting on her knees, she showed Gawion how to squeeze the clasp on both sides until it snapped open. Then she put the helmet on and leaned forward. "Try. It's plastic."

Goose pimples chased chills all over her body, at his icy touch.

Gawion, having unbuckled her helmet for the third time with hesitant, clumsy fingers, shifted his focus to her eyes. "If we succeed—"

"When we succeed," she said, with a conviction she didn't

feel. Watching him concentrate so hard on opening a clasp had not improved her confidence.

"We are already indebted to you for bringing the berries." He fiddled with his beard. "And I have something for you."

The "something" was a coin-sized tangle of hair.

In the low light, it was nearly invisible, blending in with the fur of Gawion's hand. After taking her gloves off, Tessa picked it up with thumb and forefinger, and brought it closer to her headlamp.

It wasn't a knot of hair. It was a thousand knots of hair, or the finest threads imaginable. Their intricate pattern formed a shimmering snowflake.

"Wow! It's beautiful," she whispered. In comparison, Aunt Annie's framed lace doilies were plain and lumpy.

"All snowflakes are unique wonders," Gawion said. "Maman has knotted this one of stamina."

"Stamina? Isn't that like strength or energy? How can you knot that into a snowflake?"

"Barbegazi only have little magic, but she has used strands like these." He lifted part of his beard. The pale hairs gleamed in the light. "And granted you a wish. The snowflake is a token of her promise." His nose turned the same shade of rosy pink as Mum's favorite lipstick, and he bent his head in a deep, formal bow.

"A wish? Really?" Tessa smiled despite her worries. "So, can I ask for anything? Like world peace?" she said, expecting a no. She had, after all, read lots of fairy tales.

"That is impossible," Gawion said.

"Can I visit your caves then?" She'd spent hours on the T-bar imagining cozy igloo-like domes under the snow.

"That requires Maman's permission, not magic."

"Okay, then my wish is for Maeg to be safe."

"You would do that?" Gawion frowned. "Use your wish to help us?"

She nodded.

"Thank you, but if a snowflake charm could save Maeg, Maman would have done it already."

"Let me think…" Tessa studied the knotted snowflake. If the barbegazi only had limited magic, she should wish for something smaller.

Felix knew the barbegazi existed, but she really wanted Lisa to know. Seeing Lisa's expression when she met Gawion would be priceless. Tessa could almost hear Lisa's "Oh my god," and see her cuddling the barbegazi. They'd be best friends again.

But part of her wanted to be the secret barbegazi protector. To only share the knowledge of their existence with Felix, until the time came for her own grandchild to take over the task of bringing berries.

Perhaps Lisa would like her more if she skied better in the competitions.

"Could I be the fastest tomorrow, and win the ski race?"

"Easily." Gawion grinned, showing layers of tiny pointed teeth. "You have the ability. You only lack belief in yourself. Is that your wish?"

"No. Wait. I haven't decided yet."

It would be cheating, a kind of fairy-doping. Still… Standing on the center step of the podium, holding the biggest trophy high in the air… Swishing her hair, wavy after she'd taken it out of the braids, and looking down at Lisa and Maria. Coach would slap her on the back, pleased with the points she'd gained for the team in the seasonal standings. And Mum, after being a nervous wreck while Tessa skied her run, would be so proud, and buy a winner's round of sodas for everyone.

But no, Mum wouldn't even be there. Mum might be a nervous wreck tomorrow, though not in St. Anton. She'd be in Innsbruck, in the hospital with Oma.

Tessa's excitement drained away, leaving only worry.

"There is no need to decide now," Gawion said. "Think for a day, or a year, or a decade. The wish can be fulfilled at any time."

Tessa traced the fine outline of the snowflake and nodded. She'd save the wish for something that mattered. Right now, the only thing she wanted was for Oma's broken heart to mend, and fulfilling that wish was clearly beyond barbegazi magic. After wrapping the delicate snowflake in a paper tissue, she put it in the inside breast pocket of her jacket, right next to her own heart.

That night, she lay awake long after Felix had fallen asleep. She'd not shown him the snowflake. Perhaps she never would. Under the duvet, in the light from her headlamp, she tried to follow the knotted paths of the shimmering strands. It might only be a token for a promised wish, but to her it was magical. The threads were much finer than fishing line, and much stronger. Gawion had said they were made of stamina. She still didn't understand how that was possible, but she believed him.

Clutching the snowflake, Tessa closed her eyes, and wished with all her heart that she could send some of its mysterious strength to Oma.

33

Professor Bahne

Bahne brushed his teeth until the sand ran through the hour-glass. While he flossed, he considered his incredible luck.

This was it: his chance to capture another barbegazi. With two of the creatures in his possession, it would be easy to make them talk. Despite their animal nature, they presumably had enough human characteristics to protect each other. Chimpanzees did. When he stretched the feet of one barbegazi in the rack while the other watched, the watcher would spill all their secrets.

And two barbegazi of opposite sex could be the start of an acclaimed breeding program. Science had come a long way since the middle of the nineteenth century, when the last incarcerated avalanche of barbegazi escaped, under puzzling circumstances.

He sneered, admiring the gleam on his sharp canines in the mirror.

It satisfied his need for order and patterns that his helper in finding the barbegazi was a descendant of someone who had caused him so much trouble. When he wrote *Habits & Habitats*, he was young and foolish, keen to pursue all possibilities. Now, with one sweep of his iron chain, he could overcome his regret of ever mentioning Mr. Berger.

The only two other esteemed elf researchers in Europe still ridiculed him for believing Mr. Berger's tale. Barbegazi couldn't thrive so far from the high Alps, they claimed. It was going to be an immense pleasure to prove them wrong.

His dental hygiene secured, Bahne strode to the desk. The pile of papers still lay there, and he returned them to the drawer, one by one, searching for his precious map. Its red circles indicated signs of barbegazi presence. Though most people mistook them for snowboard tracks, he never doubted when he saw their spoors.

He even suspected a barbegazi had once dug him out of an avalanche in Schöngraben. One moment he had been stuck under the white mass, the next he was inside a rescue helicopter, where a young doctor told him how lucky he was to end up on the surface of the snow. Whenever he tried to recall the location of the avalanche, however, his memory blurred, to the sound of awful music, like a ringing in the ears. So that spot was not marked on his map. His map that someone had stolen.

He slammed the drawer shut with a bang.

Was Berger's granddaughter somehow involved? If so, he might need to bring additional tools. He unlocked his suitcase and picked through the equipment inside, selecting with care.

The girl had said she kept the barbegazi a secret. That was good. Very good. If she truly saw them as her friends, she might not approve of his plans. A minor problem. After she had shown him to them, he would find a way to keep her quiet. The scientific insights to be gained were far too valuable to let such inconveniences stand in the way.

Children had accidents all the time, and the mountains were filled with dangers.

SATURDAY, DECEMBER 31

Tessa

Race day began clear and bright and freezing cold. The blue never-ending sky and the glittering mountainsides promised sunshine, but no avalanches. It had stopped snowing before midnight.

Tessa stood with her teammates, sideways, canting her skis, on the steep World Cup piste, where the best skiers in the world sometimes competed.

Coach yelled instructions on how the run should be attacked.

"You wanna come at this blue gate from above. Then quickly shift your weight for the red. Like this." He moved his bulk with surprising lightness, and cut tracks in the snow, showing the ideal curve.

One at a time, Felix first, the group followed, slowly tracing his tracks. Above and below them, other ski teams from the region, in uniform outfits, mirrored their own coaches in slow motion. Of course, they couldn't ski as close to the gates as they would in the race, and their speed was turtle-like by comparison, but it was supposed to give them a sensory memory.

Tessa's memory didn't get it. Or maybe her brain was just too full. Plan details kept popping up in her head, when she wasn't thinking about Oma. The barbegazi snowflake was back inside her breast pocket. It was silly, but she almost thought she could feel its strength and energy, like heat radiating from a tiny flame.

"Wake up, Miss My-head's-in-the-clouds!" Coach yelled.

What had Coach said? Mimicking Lisa, she trailed the others.

The race began with the youngest age groups, and Tessa went inside to drink hot chocolate with Felix, who refused to discuss the plan before the race. Afterward, in the restroom, she struggled to get her race suit up over her back protector and, in Mum's absence, had to ask a tourist for help.

When she returned to the start area, the U11 boys were already racing, and her own year group was getting ready. Some stood with their eyes closed, making slow, wavy motions with their hands, visualizing the course like World Cup skiers. Nerves bounced around, infecting everyone. Except her. Ambitious fathers shouted advice to their kids, sharpened skis, and argued over waxing techniques. Tessa's skis were in top condition— Uncle Harry had serviced them as thoroughly as Opa would've done.

Most of the mothers waited by the finish area, prepared to cheer or console. A sharp pang spasmed in her stomach. Today, Mum wasn't there to bundle her into a warm jacket and give her a hug.

Lisa made her way through the bustle. She belonged to the closed-eyes, visualizing group.

"Good luck," Tessa said.

Lisa's eyes widened.

"You too." Her mouth opened as if she wanted to say more, then closed as she gave Tessa's arm a squeeze.

"Does it help, the hand-waving thing?" Tessa asked.

Lisa shrugged. "Nah… but it makes Dad shut up." Lisa turned and wiggled out of her jacket. Her bib showed start number 113. With number 112, Tessa would be racing just ahead of her.

Uncle Harry shook her.

"Time for boots."

Tessa lifted her foot, like a horse having its hoof cleaned, and Uncle Harry scraped every single flake of snow off each boot, before he guided them into the freshly cleaned ski bindings.

Sliding her goggles on, Tessa entered the start box. Only one more minute, then she could focus on her planning. She'd never been less nervous about a race. Later today came the real challenge.

"Three push offs, Tessa! Watch the second blue. Knees!" Coach yelled. "Ready?" He held a lump of snow to the back of her bare neck. A shocking chill raced down her spine. "Steady. Go!"

Tessa pushed off, releasing the timer, and passed the first gate. In front of her, the red and blue gates made a pattern. A pattern she'd never really seen before. And suddenly it was like she was off-piste with Opa, him saying, "Look at the slope, Tessa. Decide your path." He used to drill her, forcing her to tell him her plans for a particular stretch, before they set off. Now she used the same method.

Shifting her focus from the gate immediately in front to the third gate out, made her mind concentrate on the path, not the movements. Skiing became effortless. She imagined Lisa overtaking her, even though Lisa wouldn't start until she was done. It spurred her on. The pattern continued until she passed the finish line.

Scattered cheers erupted, and a crackled voice from the loudspeaker shouted her time. She stood to the side, catching her breath. Less than a minute later, Lisa braked next to her, and the speaker's voice sounded. Both of them had times of 46 point something. The hundredths were inaudible.

"Race you to the board," Lisa said.

They clicked out of their skis and ran to the whiteboard where Karen wrote the recorded times. Tessa followed Lisa's finger to U12 girls. Their group began with number 106. Karen scribbled DNF by their last competitor with number 114. Did Not Finish. Tessa looked back at the course. Maria stood in the middle of the run with one ski in her hand, thwacking the ground with a pole.

Tessa's eyes scanned the list of numbers. Lisa had beaten her time by a mere 0.16 seconds. There were no other 46-second times, but some 47 and 48s, and a slow 53 point something. Number 108 had 45.86, and Karen circled the time with a red marker. The winner. Tessa was third. Unable to believe it, she stared at the rows of digits until Lisa congratulated her.

She'd be on the podium! Not at the very center of the podium, but right next to it. And she'd get a trophy.

Tessa crossed her fingers, wishing her luck would last the whole day. She hoped she hadn't used it all up on something as unimportant as a ski race.

35

Gawion

Three times, Gawion almost told Papa that Tessa had found Maeg. The certainty that Papa would never allow him to participate in Tessa's rescue plan held him back.

The first time was during the night, while he pretended to search for the elf hunter's vehicle with Papa. After persuading Papa that crossing the main road was too dangerous, they trudged along the mountain pass road. It was a waste of time and energy, and the only thing on Gawion's mind was Maeg. Maeg lying lifeless in an iron cage. Had she tried to protect herself by going into a deep sleep, or was it much worse?

If only they could free her now. But even if they broke the glass and entered the vehicle, they had no way of opening an iron cage. Tessa's plan was their only option. So he said nothing. And Papa was so distraught he did not notice Gawion's secret.

When the twinkling stars faded, again, he came close to telling Papa. With Papa's help, it would not take long to prepare what Tessa had envisioned. But explaining the plan and arguing with Papa might take all day. And he was running out of time.

"I feel queasy," he said. "Is that a side effect of long exposure to humans, Papa?"

As predicted, Papa sent him home at once. Guilt ate away at Gawion while he dug and scooped and scraped, preparing everything Tessa wanted.

The third time he almost told Papa was after noon. The quiet morning, resting and working in his own cave, had given him time to think. He might need his parents' help. Tessa expected them to help. The elf hunter was dangerous.

So when Papa entered his cave, he had decided to involve them. But Papa ruined everything. First, he told Gawion how he had done the floor-smoothing wrong, then he said, "No wonder your cave is a mess. You never pause to consider how to do things right."

Gawion clenched his teeth. He would show Papa about doing things right. Just wait until he rescued Maeg by himself... with a little help from his "untrustworthy" human friends.

Later, Maman came into his cave, trying to smooth over everything but the floor.

"Please come into the main cave and talk to your father," she said.

"I want to finish my room," he answered.

The moment she was out of sight, he popped halfway out of his own exit. The mechanical transporters were still emitting their metallic clanks. He waited, while the sun disappeared behind distant peaks and turned the clouds into a palette of berry colors. A pleasant wind rose, sending a refreshing mist of prickling snow across the mountainside. Before the transporter noise ceased, he took off. Alone.

It was not dark yet, but that did not worry him. His fear of normal humans paled at the thought of his looming confrontation with the elf hunter.

36

Tessa

Tessa arrived on Kapall among rattling, unoccupied chairlifts, half an hour before her meeting with Bahne. An icy wind whirled loose snow down the deserted piste and round the corner of the mountain hut. Seats of abandoned deckchairs fluttered.

After the prize-giving ceremony—Felix had of course won his race—both she and Felix had been busy getting everything organized. Luckily, Aunt Annie had been occupied in the kitchen, making finger food for a small midnight celebration, and hadn't interfered with their preparations.

Mumbling, Tessa went over elements of the plan, convincing herself she hadn't overlooked anything. Still, there was plenty to worry about. What if Bahne didn't show? What if she couldn't find the right spot? What if the barbegazi couldn't do their part? The whole project suddenly seemed like a far-fetched idea with no possible happy end.

She shivered, and decided to wait inside. The empty bar greeted her with a lingering smell of frying oil. After taking off her helmet and gloves, she perched on a bar stool. The barmaid tidied rows of snacks and gave her a peppermint tea, although the till was closed. Tessa sipped the tea. The minutes on her phone changed at an unbearably slow pace. She slipped a hand into the breast pocket of her jacket, where her fingers pierced the paper tissue so she could touch the snowflake without taking it out. Staring at the photo Felix had sent, of her on the podium, she tried to remember that feeling of being lucky from this morning.

When she went outside, Bahne stood by her skis, looking toward Schöngraben. In profile, with his bulging backpack, he resembled a hunchbacked white giant on the prowl.

He nodded in greeting, without speaking. She nodded back, opened her ski jacket and made a show of turning on her avalanche transceiver. Unzipping his jacket using long leather zipper pulls, he showed her his own blinking avalanche transceiver. Two tick marks for the plan so far. Gawion would be able to open the pockets, and they might need Bahne's transceiver for their back-up plan.

Words weren't necessary, and all she really wanted to say was: Are you ready for the revenge of the barbegazi?

She led the way past the training area, speeding up when she saw he followed. He skied well for an old man, but lacked Opa's elegant lightness.

At the boundary of the prepared piste, she hesitated. She'd promised Mum not to ski off-piste without adult supervision. Bahne was an adult. Technically, she wasn't breaking any promises, but this, if she'd asked, would surely have been forbidden.

Without giving Bahne a chance to catch his breath, she let the wind push her over the edge. If she could exhaust him, it might help.

Before the landscape fell away on the steep slope, she paused. All contours vanished in the fading light. She knew the route, but she mustn't fall. After securing her headlamp, she adjusted the beam so it pointed at the ground.

"Clever girl," Bahne wheezed, when he caught up, "I didn't think to bring mine."

Her first whistle was inaudible. She licked her frozen lips, tasting salt, and whistled again. This time, a weak tone emerged.

Two high-pitched notes answered her.

"It's them," Bahne said.

"Yes. This way."

She took the steepest incline at a slower pace. Silhouettes of lonely trees gained color when her light hit them. Her knees became springs, absorbing the bumps hidden under snowdrifts and layers of darkness.

Where the slope flattened came the tricky part: finding the exact spot. She stayed far right in the gorge, hoping the mountain stream was covered with hard snow, so that no one fell down before they were supposed to.

At the first glimpse of Gawion, she stopped. Where were his parents? She'd told him to bring them. Were they hiding? Afraid of her?

When Bahne reached her, she pointed with her pole.

Gawion waved at them.

"Hi, Tessa," he called, "Can we play?"

Bahne gasped.

"It's tame," he muttered.

"I brought someone who wants to play too." She hoped Bahne thought her voice shook because of the cold. "Go ahead, Professor."

Bahne rushed straight toward Gawion. His shadow blocked the light from Tessa's headlamp, and he glided right between the two forked twigs that stuck out of the snow and marked the hidden hollow. A moment later, as intended, the white surface collapsed under his weight. A half-choked scream preceded the sound of Bahne crashing against the ground at the bottom of the hole.

Tessa smiled and lifted both arms with ski poles over her head in triumph.

She heard a moan from the hole, before Gawion dived into a tunnel he'd already prepared. A deep clunk resonated in the hollow, as he walloped Bahne.

"Unconscious!" Gawion called. "Oh, good. It's a silver chain."

"Look for a car key in his pockets too. Pull the leather straps on his clothes. It's probably a square, black plastic thing," she called, not daring to move closer to the trap.

Moments later, Gawion appeared out of the snow next to Tessa, and handed her a car key and the silver chain. Of the three keys on the chain, one was old fashioned and heavy, with a rusted wavy pattern around the large hole. The other two looked like normal padlock keys. After she dropped all of them into her pocket, she zipped it, and double checked that it was closed. Under no circumstances could she lose these keys.

So far, everything had gone as planned. She had the keys to the cage. Bahne lay unconscious in the hole. Gawion was in control of him.

Dad always said "Fortune favors the bold." With such a bold plan, perhaps she'd stay lucky.

37

Gawion

After Tessa left, Gawion walloped the elf hunter again, as a safety precaution.

It half-sat, leaning against the thing on its back, with its head drooping to the side. He opened the buckle under its beardless chin and removed the shell. By pulling on the plastic handles, he wiggled the sticks away from its hands. The wooden feet lay disconnected from the human. He avoided touching them. If only he did not have to touch the foul creature. Its faint whiff of thawing spring snow had disappeared. Now it only reeked of iron.

Standing over the human, Gawion rehearsed the memory alteration, mumbling, "Cover the eyes with my beard, touch the temples with all six fingertips, erase memories by speaking the charm three times, then say it backward to seed replacement memories."

Although Papa had taught him the charm decades ago, he still lacked understanding of that last bit. It replaced the original memories with snippets of the awful noise that blasted from human dens on the mountain every afternoon. Somehow, this particular kind of noise matched the befuddled state of the humans just after they had been charmed. When he had told Tessa, it laughed and said "That's why I felt so funny, and kept hearing après-ski songs in my head."

He had nodded as if the explanation made sense.

Gawion had altered memories several times on his own, but he had never tried to erase such a long period of time: six days and five nights. And his last memory charm was a disaster—Tessa had remembered him asking about the berry gift. Perhaps he should have listened and involved his parents. If he failed to remove all six days' memories, the elf hunter remained a threat. The elf hunter! Its stench alone made him sick.

He hated what it had done to his sister. How it had made her suffer. Her time in captivity would torment Maeg for the rest of her long life, while this evil creature would remember nothing.

Ice-cold rage filled him. His fingers tingled. Tiny icicles grew at the end of his claws, and ice crystals appeared on the elf hunter's hair and eyebrows and wispy mustache.

Altering its memory, making it forget everything, was not enough. He wanted the human to know that everything it had achieved—the fulfilment of its lifelong dream of capturing a barbegazi—had been taken away. Of course, it would remember nothing after Gawion's charm. But at least in that one moment, when it realized everything was lost, it would suffer.

So he did not alter its memory right away. Instead, he sat down and waited for the human to gain consciousness.

At its first moan, Gawion stood. He paced along the circular wall until it stirred, then he said, "Elf hunter!"

"Mmmm... hmmm... yes?"

"My dear sister, whom you have captured, is being freed."

"Mmmm... How?" Its head rolled forward. A hand rose to its neck, searching for the chain. "The clever girl," it said very slowly.

"Oh, yes. My friend is very clever." Gawion continued his walk of the perimeter. He felt invincible, with the elf hunter in his power. "While we wait, I shall be a real fairy and grant you answers to three questions."

"Three questions?" The elf hunter raised its head, looking for him in the gloom. "But barbegazi are not fairies."

"Fairy, elf, or human—why does everyone focus on our differences?" he grumbled. Perhaps he had overplayed his role. Been too nice. He would speak in a tone it could understand.

"Yes, three questions. And that was the answer to your first question. You have two left."

"Sustenance. What do you need?" it asked without hesitation, sitting upright.

"That is an easy one. We thrive on frozen forest berries. They contain all the nutrients we need. As they discovered in Vienna..." Gawion threw this last comment to the elf hunter, like a fisher-human throws a line and hook. He had seen that once, when he was little. The desperate screams of the impaled trout still haunted him in daymares.

"The zookeeper's daughter…" the human said. "That wasn't a question."

Gawion flexed his fingers. Toying with the elf hunter gave him no satisfaction. Even though it was still weak, he should probably wallop it again.

"If you really are part of the Vienna avalanche of barbegazi, why stop here, when you are more than halfway to the high Alps and their expansive glaciers?"

"My mother was too pregnant to continue," he said, not bothering with a more detailed answer. "Are you happy, now you know everything?"

The human squirmed, but stayed silent.

"In a few moments, you will know nothing." Gawion arched his soles and bounced lightly on his heels. He stood three barbegazi feet from the human's head. The exact distance for a perfect leap.

The elf hunter's eyes roamed, searching for him. But to human eyes, in this weak light and standing in front of a snow wall, Gawion was almost invisible.

"I am going to alter your memory. Afterward, you will not remember having seen either me or my sister, and the clever girl will be just another irritating human child."

The elf hunter still did not speak.

Gawion searched for signs of suffering or remorse in its stern features. To his disappointment, he found none.

With a hard rebound of his heels, he leapt with his arm outstretched. But the elf hunter pulled something out from behind itself, and swung it upward. It connected with Gawion's arm. A metallic *plink* sounded. Gawion screamed. He landed on the wooden feet, burning his hip. Fire spread down his leg and up to his ribs. His walloping arm felt heavy and numb.

The elf hunter swung its long animal-skin strap with the metal buckle again. With immense effort, Gawion pushed off with his uninjured hand and rolled away until he hit the wall of snow.

The human dislodged the pack from its back and scrambled up. While it continued to swing the strap, it rummaged in the pack.

Gawion had just sprung to his feet, when it withdrew a long, rattling chain. The foul smell of iron invaded his nostrils.

Brandishing the iron chain in one hand, and swinging the strap in circles with the other, the elf hunter advanced toward him.

Gawion pressed himself against the wall, unsure which way to move. Left or right? Could he jump over this tall human?

The elf hunter sneered.

"Did you think I would come unprepared? Without iron?"

38

Tessa

Seconds after Tessa flashed her headlamp toward Felix's window, he came running out of the house, in his ski jacket, with normal boots for her and Mum's big rucksack, to carry Maeg in. Between gasps of breath, while she changed boots, she told him what had happened. She left her skiing stuff under the large pine tree, before they set off on their mountain bikes.

Despite the scattered gravel, they skidded on frozen puddles in every turn of the narrow village roads. Tessa kept one foot on the ground and glided more than she pedaled. She was grateful to be wearing her ski helmet and back protector.

By the hiking trail, they dismounted and abandoned the bikes. As they jogged up to the sawmill, the lights from their headlamps bounced on the stacked timber like glow-in-the-dark rubber balls.

The deep-frozen van still stood behind the shed. Tessa made a mental tick mark. She listened. Blood pounded in her ears. She heard nothing else. No long-distance barbegazi whistle yet. It worried her. Gawion had promised to signal when it was done, and he'd assured her the sound would be audible throughout the valley. Had he overestimated his own abilities?

After she extracted the keys from her pocket, she unlocked the van, wincing at the high beep it made.

"Give me the berries."

"Berries!" Felix hit his forehead, making his light disappear. "I forgot. Sorry, Tessa."

"Never mind. We'll stop and get some from Oma's freezer." Her house keys clanked, reassuring her, when she patted her pocket.

Inside, she crawled across the seats to the back, calling to Maeg. The bundle of fur didn't stir. A terrible thought struck her.

Could Maeg be dead?

Tessa crouched by the cage, her head bent to stay clear of the ceiling. Her hands shook, and she dropped the set of keys twice, before she managed to open the two padlocks with the modern keys. Clanking against the bars of the cage, the iron chains slithered down.

The keyhole of the lock on the cage door was rusty, and the big old-fashioned key wouldn't turn. Water dripped onto her fingers—a mixture of melting snow, sweat, and tears of frustration.

"Help me, Felix," she screeched.

He pushed her aside and bent down there for a while, wiggling and jiggling the mechanism until something clicked, and the key turned. After he opened the hatch, Tessa crawled into the small space. She shook Maeg gently and searched for a pulse. Not even the slightest vibration quivered in the barbegazi's lifeless body.

Iron bars on the floor cut into Tessa's knees. Maeg had lain on them all week. No wonder she was paralyzed.

"Is she hibernating?" Tessa asked, but of course she knew barbegazi slept during the summer.

Carefully, she scooped the limp body up and backed out of the iron cage. Maeg's lightness surprised her—she weighed less than Lisa's cat. Felix stood outside, and she handed Maeg to him, before she jumped to the ground.

"Let's get her in the rucksack." Felix handled the fur bundle like Oma handled the china she'd inherited from her own grandmother.

They quickly discovered, however, that they couldn't get Maeg into the rucksack without her sinking to the bottom, where she wouldn't be able to breathe. If she still needed to breathe.

But if they carried her in their arms, they'd be walking through the village with a barbegazi in plain sight! And they'd be moving much slower than on their bikes. If only they could get a ride in a car. If only—

"Come on, Tessa. We have to go."

"One sec. I have to think." She closed her eyes. The sound of a passing car on the main road could be heard above the noise from the river. No whistles.

There was something she'd overlooked. It was something

about a car. Mum's car? Uncle Harry's car? No. The professor's car… His van, right here in the deserted sawmill.

Suddenly she realized there was a hole in her plan.

"If Gawion succeeds…" At the twinge of doubt, she crossed her fingers for luck. "Bahne's memory will be wiped of everything that has happened this week. He'll not remember where he parked."

"Can't we just tell him? Or call the police about a stolen vehicle, like in the back-up plan?"

"No. We don't want him to be suspicious. I broke through Gawion's memory charm. In a dream. Without trying to." Gawion had told her the barbegazi only had little magic. He still hadn't whistled. What if, while they freed Maeg, Bahne captured her family?

How could she have ever imagined this plan would work? Her brilliant plan had a gaping hole, and that hole was growing into an abyss.

Tessa's luck had run out.

"What do we do?" she said, not even trying to hide her panic.

39

Gawion

The iron chain and the metal buckle swung toward him. Gawion's eyes followed them as the elf hunter drew nearer. Left or right? Over or under? Forward or—

He swirled and dived backward into the wall of snow. His enormous, long feet paddled in the air like parallel wings. They propelled him deep into crusty snow. He had escaped.

"Ow!" A hard slap, followed by a stinging, burning pain, traveled the length of his left foot and up his leg. He thrashed with his right foot, digging and sending a spray of icy crystals backward. But no matter how much he kicked, he could not move forward. Something was holding him back. And he felt weaker.

He continued spraying snow behind him while he enlarged the tunnel with his uninjured hand. And then, looking back, he saw the iron chain. Looped round his left foot, it bit deep into his fur. Even worse, it must be digging into the sensitive skin of his soles. The taut chain stretched out of the tunnel into a pair of human hands, just visible in the hole.

He tried to wiggle out of the chain—it was not fastened—but his foot did not respond. His whole leg was now as sore as his walloping arm. If he used his good hand to remove the chain, he would be left with only one functioning limb. But if he made the chain go slack, it might loosen the hold on his foot. As much as he hated the idea, he had to move back, toward the elf hunter.

Gawion kicked violently with his right leg, pushing a load of icy snow at the human. Then he shifted the angle of his left leg and paddled backward. He slapped the elf hunter's head with his good foot before he pulled himself back into the tunnel. Had it worked? His left foot remained senseless, but he kept going, unsure of his success until his hand met the hard crust immediately below the surface.

Not completely on purpose, he had dug a zigzagging tunnel—controlling direction with one leg was difficult. When he emerged above the snow, he lay for a while, massaging his left foot with lumps of icy flakes. His walloping arm throbbed and prickled, like the time he had fallen over a cliff into a cluster of snow-dusted brambles. If only he had some blackberries to restore his energy.

"Barbegazi!" the elf hunter called from the hole nearby. "If you help me out of here, I will not harm you. And I will let your sister go."

As if it had any bargaining power! Gawion stood up on his good leg. His injured foot still burned. When he set it down on the snow, it prickled worse than those thorns from the brambles, and the leg collapsed under his weight. Somehow he stayed standing.

Perhaps he could imitate the strange one-wooden-footed humans he had seen surfing sideways on the slopes.

"Tessa has freed my sister," he said. Had Tessa freed Maeg? Was it waiting for his signal? He could whistle now. That was bound to bring Papa. But his task was not done yet, and if he could manage to complete it without Papa's help… His walloping arm did feel a lot better.

Hopping around on one foot exposed him, so he let himself fall forward. On his stomach, he wiggled to the hole and peeked over the rim.

The metal buckle, with its animal-skin tail, whizzed past his ear.

"Try again, elf hunter!" he called, hoping to goad it into hurling the iron chain.

The human swung the chain. Gawion clambered back. The chain dug into the overhanging snow, tearing fluffy chunks down over the human.

Unfortunately, it was not foolish enough to let go of the chain.

He crept back to the rim. The human stood in the center—swinging the chain, turning slowly, staring at the top of the walls—prepared for an attack.

Gawion retreated and dug a short tunnel that stopped just before breaking into the hole. After he returned to the surface, he watched the human make five turns, while he counted in his head.

The elf hunter made one fatal mistake: it kept the speed and direction of its turning constant.

Gawion, still counting, dived into the prepared tunnel and out through the thin snow barrier. With a forceful swipe of his recovered arm, he walloped the elf hunter from behind.

This time he proceeded without hesitation. While he spoke the charm, his fingertips pushed against its temples and his beard hid its stunned expression. A pleasant tingle traveled up his arms, as the elf hunter's recent memories evaporated.

FROM *HABITS & HABITATS: A HISTORIC ACCOUNT OF ALPINE ELVES* BY PROFESSOR DR. EBERHART LUDWIG FRITZ BAHNE

The only known instance of barbegazi surviving more than a few weeks in captivity is recorded by a zookeeper's daughter in Vienna's Tiergarten Schönbrunn.

In a diary entry from January 1862, the girl, Anne, mentions that the avalanche of barbegazi, which had been in the zoological gardens since shortly after the opening of the imperial menagerie in 1752, had escaped during a blizzard.

No one understood how their barred iron cage had been opened. I, of course, revealed nothing, she writes, leading to a belief that she had a hand in their escape.

A February entry strengthens suspicions of a conspiracy. *As I promised Aeglosben, I have destroyed the barbegazi notebooks my father inherited from his predecessors.*

This blatant disregard for unique scientific insight explains why no accounts have been found of where the barbegazi were kept during the summer months, or their dietary needs.

—40—

Tessa

"I'll get Dad to tell the professor where he parked," Felix said. "We'll invent a reason. Just come on, Tessa."

The adrenaline that had surged through her body all day was used up. The light bundle in her arms had become as heavy as her tired legs. She couldn't face running all the way back to the main road and uphill through the village to Felix's house. And what if the sight that met them there was a sneering elf hunter, with a chain around an avalanche of barbegazi?

"Now." Felix pulled at her sleeve.

They really had to go. She took two tentative steps.

Just then, a piercing whistle reverberated in the valley.

She looked up at Felix.

It was Gawion's whistle. He had succeeded!

The shrill sound roused her. In seconds, her brain filled the gaping hole in her plan with possible solutions. One of them just might work.

Words tumbled out of her mouth: "You have that racing-car

computer game, right? And you help your grandfather with the harvest. You can drive a tractor, can't you?"

"What're you getting at?" Felix looked back at the van. "No way. If I scratch it... Oh, man..." Holding his hands up, he took rapid breaths. "Okay, I'll try, okay? But no one can see us."

"They won't. Tinted windows, remember?"

They sprinted to the van. Its engine roared when Felix pressed a button. He adjusted the seat and surveyed the knobs and levers. His hands gripped the steering wheel, the strain visible on his white knuckles, in the light from the instrument panel. Tessa relaxed her own grip on the cold body she was holding, and cradled Maeg in her arms.

"Here goes," Felix muttered. The vehicle sprang forward and rolled along the track out of the old sawmill. Where the track ended, he hesitated before he slowly drove up the main road, staring straight ahead. A car behind them honked. When they turned onto the steep curving road to the village, it didn't follow.

"We need to get the berries from my house," Tessa said.

"No, Tessa. I'm sure Mum has—"

"And you're going to march in and take them?"

Felix didn't answer, but drove down Tessa's street.

"Be quick," he said, as she opened the door.

Leaving Maeg on her seat, she ran to the house, pulling the keys from her pocket. She entered, and, without closing the door, without turning on the lights, ran downstairs in her boots and grabbed a bag of mixed forest berries.

It was only after she had closed the freezer that she noticed the absolute silence. The ticks from the grandfather clock had stopped. No one had been winding it, that was all—surely it meant nothing else. Her fingers found the hole in the paper tissue and touched the snowflake, then she took a deep breath, willing the wave of fear away.

Outside, Felix had turned the vehicle around, and she'd just reached it when someone called, "Tes-sa!"

By the first house on Tessa's street, stood Lisa. With Maria. "We wanted to ask if you—"

"I don't have time now," Tessa shouted. She jumped inside while Felix lifted Maeg. "Go. Just go," she said, taking the fur bundle and hugging it to her chest.

"Hey! Isn't that the van…" The rest of what Lisa was saying was drowned out as Felix accelerated up the street.

Without scratching anything, Felix parked behind his house, by the large pine tree. Gawion wasn't there yet. They sat in silence for a moment, the lifeless bundle warm in Tessa's arms. The few times Gawion had touched her, the icy shock had given her goose pimples.

"She's not cold," Tessa screamed. She sprang out of the van, placed Maeg on the white ground underneath the tree, and began scooping snow over her. They had to cool her down if they were going to find a spark of life and revive her.

If there was life.

"Let me do that," Felix said. "Give her some berries."

Tessa pushed Maeg's beard aside and tried to squeeze a berry into her mouth. A tiny blueberry made it through her clenched lips.

Nothing happened.

Frantically, Felix packed more snow around the small creature. Tessa spilled berries out onto the ground, in her haste to find another miniature one.

"Why's nothing happening? We're too late, Felix!" she said, sinking back on her heels.

Maeg's eyelids fluttered.

They watched, holding their breath, as she swallowed the blueberry.

Tessa exhaled. Maeg was alive.

The little mouth opened and closed, like a baby's searching for milk, and Tessa fed berries into it.

"Maeg," she whispered. "Don't be afraid. Gawion will be here soon."

Maeg blinked. In the gloomy light her dark eyes darted back and forth between Tessa and Felix. Faster than Tessa could feed her, she devoured the berries.

Close by, they heard running footsteps and Lisa calling out.

"Tes-sa! Where are you? Are you okay?" She had stopped by the van in a spot where the twigs didn't quite cover their hiding place.

They scrambled to sit in front of the barbegazi, and the sucking noises she'd made ceased. Tessa got up by putting a hand on Felix's shoulder. She pushed him slightly backward, and hoped he understood that he had to stay and shield Maeg.

Careful to block the opening to their shelter, she pushed through the branches out to Lisa.

"Where's Maria?"

"Waiting for me by the bus stop. What're you doing in there?" Lisa craned her neck to peek behind Tessa.

Could she trust her? She'd so wanted for Lisa to believe her. It would be amazing if they could share the secret of the barbegazi and become best friends again.

But Gawion trusted her. And she trusted herself, now that she knew the barbegazi existed. Perhaps that was enough. Perhaps that was why Opa had never cared if people laughed at him behind his back. Because it was enough that he knew.

"It's nothing," she said. "Just a little surprise for a guest."

Lisa pointed.

"And the van—"

"Has been found," Tessa interrupted. "Thanks for looking for it. Anyway—"

"D'you want to come to my house? We can watch the fireworks together."

"What? Now?" Lisa couldn't have picked a worse time. Why now? Was it because she'd been on the podium? "I have to finish this, erm…"

"Or tomorrow. Whenever you want. I'll even help you look for those elves."

"Maybe. Thanks." It would be so easy to show Maeg to Lisa.

"Bye then…" Lisa's hand rested on Tessa's arm, before she turned and walked away.

Tessa looked after her until she rounded the corner.

As soon as Lisa was gone, a low whistle sounded nearby.

From underneath the tree, Maeg whistled in answer.

Felix crawled out into the open, gasping, and the strangest thing Tessa had ever seen came into view, behind him. Gawion and another barbegazi carried the professor on their shoulders, as if he were a decaying log. They also threw him on the ground like a log, and Bahne rolled twice before coming to a stop by his van's back wheels.

"Out of my sight, elf hunter," said a voice much deeper than Gawion's. The stocky barbegazi cast a fleeting glance at them before he ducked under the branches of the pine tree.

"Papa," Maeg peeped.

Gawion smiled. "The elf hunter's heavy," he said, nodding toward the white heap. "Good thing Papa came when I whistled my long-distance signal."

A bark announced the arrival of Brownie. Gawion answered with barks of his own.

"Good dog." Felix rubbed the big dog's pleated neck.

Brownie and Gawion barked some short laughter-like coughs, and Felix stared open-mouthed from one to the other.

When Gawion barked again, Brownie sped off.

"What did you tell him? I've never seen him run so fast," Tessa said.

"I wanted to present him to my father. But Papa is fearful of dogs, and I might have confused the barks for scared and scary." Gawion shook his head. "The local Dog dialect is tricky…"

Bahne moaned.

"We'd better get him away from here," Felix said. "Help me, Tessa."

Somehow they got the professor upright. He was humming a tune. Tessa sneaked the chain over his head, and Felix put the car key back in his pocket, while they supported him to the front door.

Bahne sang out a few lines from "Take Me Home, Country Road" and hiccupped.

At the top of the steps, they let go, and he slumped, then slid down onto the bottom step. Felix rang the doorbell until Aunt Annie appeared.

"What's this racket?" She saw Bahne and frowned.

He leaned against the steps and bent his head back until he could see her upside-down, then he broke out in song again.

"Mr. Bahne," Aunt Annie said, her cheeks flushing a deep red. "I had not expected this kind of behavior from you." She marched down and tugged hard on his arm. "Felix, let's get this drunk to his room."

Tessa watched them hobble up the stairs. Aunt Annie was ranting about alcohol, and skis being stolen if you left them outside bars, and proper behavior. Bahne kept humming and singing. His voice wasn't bad.

Just as she started back toward Gawion from the front steps, a car pulled up next to her. Mum jumped out and hugged her, laughing and crying at the same time.

"It's a miracle," she squealed. "Oma's so much better. She

might not even need the surgery." Mum held Tessa in her out-stretched arms and smiled. "Your little crossword puzzle cheered her up immensely! Perhaps you can make her another?"

Tessa nodded and wiped a tear away. In her mind, she began laying Scrabble tiles for *barbegazi, rescue, snowflake, stamina,* and all the other things she wanted Oma to know. Fitting everything into one secret message was going to be difficult.

"Then you can give it to her when she comes home on Monday."

"On Monday?" Tessa felt a smile growing across her face. She hugged Mum tight.

Gawion was waving to Tessa, from where he stood by the pine. He waved her closer. Behind Mum's back, Tessa made hand signals, trying to gauge whether Mum was allowed to see him. He nodded.

"Come," Mum said, taking Tessa's hand, "Let's go inside and give Annie the good news."

"I'll be right there, Mum. I just have to say goodbye to the barbegazi."

Mum's face fell.

"Tessa, no. Don't start that again."

Tessa swung Mum around, so she faced Gawion.

Mum just stared at him.

"Another miracle," she mumbled.

Tessa ran over to Gawion, crouched and embraced him.

"Thank you," she said, trying to cram all her happiness into those two words.

"Thank you, Tessa. Papa said I can bring you to see our caves." Gawion clung to her, making her shiver with cold. "If you had not found us, Maeg would not have survived."

She drew back, new anxiety rising inside her.

"But what if other humans find you?"

"Just bring them to me. I am getting quite adept at memory charms."

Tessa giggled. Part of being a secret barbegazi protector meant she'd become a specialized mountain guide. The kind who arranged covert excursions for people who knew about the barbegazi. Until suddenly they didn't.

Above them, the sky exploded in red sparkles. The year was ending, but not the winter. Tomorrow she'd visit their caves, and, before the snow melted and the barbegazi hid away to aestivate, surely she'd see Gawion surf on an avalanche.

Acknowledgments

I'm immensely grateful to Sarah Odedina for her encouragement and high expectations during the last couple of years, and for helping me find and shape the heart of this story. To Tilda Johnson for her thoughtful line and copy edits. And to the wonderful team at Pushkin Press for transforming my barbegazi tale into a beautiful book. Many thanks also to Allison Hellegers at Rights People and Mari Kesselring and everyone at Jolly Fish Press for bringing the story to North American readers, and to Aubrey Blackham for the stunning cover.

Massive thanks to my friends in SCBWI, Cafe Schreiber in Zurich and The Singapore Writers' Group for helping me learn and grow as a writer. I'm especially indebted to my early readers and those who listened to my endless barbegazi monologues: Jo Furniss, Sherida Deeprose, Helena Ryan, Rebecca Foreman, Catherine Carvell, Emma Nicholson, Annette Woschek and Dorte Sidelmann Rossen. A special thanks to the Asian Festival of Children's Content for creating inspiring conferences and providing brilliant opportunities for writers and illustrators, such as the one that connected me with Sarah Odedina.

An avalanche of hugs to the dedicated ski coaches, enthusiastic parents and tireless ski-club kids from my time in

Trainingsgemeinschaft Stanzertal and all my other friends in St. Anton. This book would not exist if I had not spent hours on the Schöngraben T-bar lift, watching my sons at race practice and gazing at the white wilderness (without binoculars), daydreaming about encounters with fantastical creatures. Any resemblance to real people and buildings is purely coincidental, but I have tried to stay faithful to the wondrous landscape on Arlberg, with the minor addition of a small glacier in the vicinity.

Last, but not least, infinite thanks to my father, who raised me to believe I could do anything, and my mother, who fed me fairy tales and passed her love of books on to me. To Marcus, who heard about this story first, for his suggestions, and August, who read it first, for his ski racing insights. Finally, to Claus, my teammate in life, who listens to all my implausible plans and supports most of them. Even when I had doubts, he always believed in my dream of becoming an author.